SHORT SESSION

Bill O'Neill

ISBN 978-1-952204-04-3
Printed in the United States of America

RED MOUNTAIN PRESS
Seattle, Washington
www.redmountainpress.us

For Joe Christmas

.

Ever tried. Ever failed. No matter. Try again. Fail again. Fail better.

— *Samuel Beckett*

Nothing is more important than getting the politics right. Nothing.

—*Charles Krauthammer*

Acknowledgements

Much gratitude, as always, to my very patient and demanding editor, Susan Gardner, who endures my shortcomings and still believes in my work. Also, to the technical assistance provided by my friends Holly Velazquez-Duffy and Rachel Gudgel. And to the great State of New Mexico, with its colorful and mostly well-intentioned political tradition.

Bill O'Neill
New Mexico State Senator
Albuquerque, NM
July 2020

1

I should clarify that I was not exactly *invited* to run for State Senate District 10: people like me, who feel such an urge or calling, do not need to be prodded. We are alert to the opportunity when it presents itself—an incumbent retiring, a new district created courtesy of gerrymandering, a bad vote. There is always the justification, deep down, that we can do a better a job. That we belong in that role instead. In my case, I need to also admit that my reasons for declaring were less than pure. I wanted to play in the House/Senate Charity Basketball Game, I admit it. This annual event, complete with uniforms, coaches, announcers, referees, cheerleaders, played in front of a nearly full high-school gymnasium, a band even—all proceeds to the local homeless shelter—had me imagining what *I* could do if given the opportunity to play. You had to be a legislator in order to play. No staff, no lobbyists, no former Governors. Each chamber represented one of the two dueling state universities, which plugged into that rivalry as well. I had visions of how many baskets I could score, three-pointers as well. But I needed to be elected first.

And then there was the red license plate, which represented the other reason why I decided to run for office. I have no idea why possessing the honor of that license plate had such a pull for me, it just did. Affirmation maybe in the form of the embossed *Senator* lettering? Or simply how nice it would look on my black car? Some kind of compensatory symbol for my lost decades?

Of course, once my electoral journey began, these original reasons began to fade into something more mature, more fitting of public service. In fairness, running for office did represent a logical progression for me: student council president, delegate to Iowa Boys State, summer Congressional Intern, some forgotten student officer position at Brown. And from my first visit to the legislature—on behalf of Hope House, of course—I was smitten. The celestial light streaming down from our stories-high Capitol dome onto the Rotunda's marble inlaid floor and its incomprehensible state slogan, how best dressed and *nice* everyone was, as you did not really know who anyone was.

My mission was to secure Corrections Department funding for the Cadillac of halfway houses, Hope House. To that end, I quickly learned the more rudimentary protocols: present your card to the attendant and wait patiently behind the clearly marked sign, be nice to everyone because who knows who they are, when the legislator does emerge have your elevator speech game tight, and *never* venture onto the chamber floor while they are in session. But on a deeper level, I immediately felt that I belonged here in this stunningly beautiful building, art everywhere on the walls of its many hallways, and doing the important work of keeping our tenuous charity solvent. And, in a maybe presumptuous way, thinking that I could perhaps, one day, be on the other side of that aforementioned line. Learn to speak in a more formal cadence, through the chair of course. Sponsor bills. Suit up for the game.

And, reader of the newspaper that I was, I sensed an opportunity in the upcoming presidential election year. When no other Democratic challenger emerged, I hurriedly moved into the district on the last possible day and filed the necessary paperwork with the local county clerk. My friend gave me a room in the back of her house, and this was my new address. I was surprised, however, to learn that I was not registered as a Democrat (Independent I was), and my soon-to-be friend at the county desk looked at me with more than a faint smile.

"It might help to know what party you are in," Sisto teased.

"This is all new to me," I answered.

"Apparently," he replied.

"I just didn't vote much back in the 90's,"I continued.

"I wouldn't let your opponent know that," he answered, "if I were you. Though if they take you seriously, they will let that be known."

I then did my best to clear it with my Hope House board— it would take the form of a leave of absence, which could maybe help with our program's visibility, as who does not appreciate the struggles of criminal offenders trying to go straight? Well, it worked for me at least, the time off, a kind of break, it being Spring. And soon I was at the doorsteps, checking for evidence of a dog in the yard, waiting for the door to open, my clipboard in hand and ready with my pitch. And how to convey the beauty of going door to door? The voter flattered by your visit, once he understands that sales or a religious conversion is not in play, just two people talking about how we can make our state a better place to live? Partisan affiliation fading in the bright Saturday afternoon light, closing with a non-committal "Just keep me in mind?" request on my end, and the usual "I will definitely *keep you in mind*" response.

"Chapman, what is up, bro?" It was Santiago. "Why so down, *ese*?"

"Am I that transparent?" I replied to my thin, energetic colleague of the hallways.

"You're easy to read. Your face, and I'm even younger than you."

"Yeah, but your day of reckoning is coming."

"You look good for an old man. Why so bitter?"

"I am *not* bitter. I just don't like birthdays, that's all. My own, I mean. You got any bills today?"

"Eeeh, a ton."

"It's better to keep busy, isn't it?"

"I am not complaining. It's just that I can't get any sleep." Santiago winked at me as a pretty young staffer went by.

"Stop hanging out in the bars then," I scolded him. "That's all this place is."

"It's part of the job, *ese*. These functions, these parties. And the girls."

"I thought you were in a relationship."

"I am," he replied. "It's just that it's full on up here, all the time."

"I come up here, do my business, then leave."

"Dude. I have seen you out. Plenty of times."

"Whatever."

"Too bad you lost. It was close, wasn't it? A couple hundred votes?"

"More like nine hundred. But hey, 'razor-thin' it was."

"Not a good year to be a Democrat. But you didn't get stomped, like the other gringo."

"I suppose … anyway," I really did not want to talk about my stupid election anymore, "that was some food you had the other night."

"You mean at our Super Bowl Party?"

"Yeah, what was that? Deer or moose meat or something?"

"Elk. It's a tradition up north and whatnot."

"Anyway, keep me on your invite list. I'll actually attend your things."

"Oh, then we will be honored—especially because of your self-denial and whatnot."

"No, seriously. That was an excellent party."

"Are you going to run again?"

"My foot hurts."

"Seriously."

We were in my favorite hallway, with the light just right, the Zozobra triptych guiding our thoughts and actions. Judiciary

Committee soon to start, once the House members were off the floor. The waiting. It's what we do.

"Are you going to give me fifteen thousand dollars?" I answered Santiago's question. "I have campaign debt, you know."

"Sure, buddy. Just let me make some calls."

"Get out of here, man. I was enjoying my privacy."

"This is a good bench, eh?" he asked, winking again. "I mean *location wise.*"

"Enough of that," I replied immediately. "I'm in a relationship too. As men, we can be better than we are."

"Okay," he said evenly. "I buy that. But a man can look." We were both silent as an attractive lobbyist walked swiftly by, probably late for the floor session. We did not look at each other. "No matter what his situation might be," Santiago concluded.

"Look, I am not scolding anyone. I am just more aware of these things—as I get older. "

"There you go again."

"Actually, though, I've always been like that. Since my first girlfriend."

"I love this building, " Santiago interjected. "I mean, it's all nice and polished," he added, looking over towards the Rotunda.

"And the artwork," I pointed out. "It's like a freakin' museum."

"And the wood," Santiago added. "I mean, where did they find that? It's not indigenous."

"What do you think of the art?"

"Yeah, that too. As a native New Mexican, I am proud of our State Capitol. I don't care how much they spent. It belongs to the people. *La gente.*"

"It was millions—a billion even?"

"So what?"

"Talk to the Republicans."

"They're the minority here, *hermano.*"

"Not in my district."

"They should not have carved it up like that. That used to be the Senator's fiefdom. Back in the day, you get the nomination, and you're in. "

"Maybe that's why I didn't have a primary."

"*No es verdad.* I know people who looked at it."

"Whatever."

"You ran well. The Irish tenacious one."

"My foot hurts."

"Anyway, later on, man. House Judiciary should be starting soon. They gotta be off the floor by now."

"Good luck." We shook hands, and I remained seated.

"Let's continue this," Santiago added. "I mean about the other business, the personal stuff. I'm kind of dealing with some things now,"

"Okay, guy."

I went back to the fund-raising, and the daily drama of Hope House, which should not have been my concern, given that my role had become clearly defined: *get the money … and no need to become entangled with the daily struggle of my beloved parolees.* When I returned, after however long I was on the freights— my version of getting clear—Salazar, my board president and best friend, was ecstatic:

"Chappie," he said. "You are back. You have come to your senses."

"Dude," I replied. "A month on the trains takes it out of a person. Understandably."

"We have hope now. Here at the Hope House."

"It's all we have, man."

"No," he continued. "We are in trouble. Financially."

"We are always in trouble."

"Your leaving did not exactly help."

"How much do we have in the bank?" I asked.

"Not enough."

"Can we cover next month? I mean, for utilities, salaries …"

"We like our new hire. Have you met her yet?"

"No."

"Now, we were real clear with her. Just to let you do your quirky thing. That you need a lot of space. That you hate meetings— "

"Where souls go to die."

"That the bottom line with you is delivering the private donations. And of course, our annual event. She can do the grants. Has a master's in business, I think, or some such thing. Written many grants, she has."

"Do I report to her?"

"No. We have taken care of that. You report to our Finance Committee."

"I am allowed to visit the house?"

"Come on, man. Those days are over."

"The memory lingers."

"Just do your thing, like you do. In the community and all of that." Salazar paused. "And no secret loans to residents. Which obviously do not remain secret for very long. You are white collar now, guy. A fund-raising professional."

"I still have to go to those United Way things?" I asked.

"Come on. You get a free meal out of it. You've got to meet people where they are. We've talked about this," Salazar added with some impatience.

"Okay."

"You'll like her," Salazar continued. "I promise."

"How old is she?"

"Close to you in age, I think. How old are you anyway?"

"Counting my lost decade?"

"Everything counts."

"Thirty-three."

"My God. You're just a kid."

"Whatever."

My reunion with Hope House went much better than my return to Kit, which I will get into later. And it was back to facing the relentless demand of fund-raising, which at least I could do on my own terms, the past personnel dramas increasingly a memory. I could play as much noontime basketball as I wanted, could keep my office off-site as well, as long as the monthly revenue was *there*. And then there gradually emerged this potential of state funding, which surely, we deserved, as we were all crime-fighters deep down, our mission to reclaim individuals from thievery and worse. We could bring our idealism to the State Capitol, for that period of time at least, and clearly, we could legislate and govern into a better world, right? And yes, being young—if I can still claim that defect—the opposite sex so attractive, alluring, full of possibility, which of course would remain just that, possibility. This important work of Hope House, to be acknowledged for the public service we provide, should, at least, give us some breathing room. If someone does not re-offend, then are we not a safer community? And though this hustler-for-good role of mine seems to be have become a natural fit, I do grow weary of having to scrape by every year depending upon the mercy or kindly impulse of others. It can be a hard sell, when competing with the other more noble charities—the wounded, the disadvantaged, the disabled; will you please consider donating to a cause that helps the thief who burglarized your house last month? The drug addict that stole your car?

But thank goodness for the churches, with their message of forgiveness and attending to the least of our brothers and sisters. And also, for the criminal defense attorneys—and their cousins in the same profession—as I methodically worked through the Bar Directory, dropping the name of the last unfortunate attorney who had just written a check in their bustling office. And to the parties I went, trying to restrain myself from my inevitable agenda with all who are relaxing and maybe sipping champagne (especially that one holiday bash, oh man). But always overdoing it, I can tell by reading their faces, the hesitation in conversation as I approach their trio. The follow-ups were always awkward, like getting through that first secretary: "Is Mr. Padilla in today?"(Of course, he is, as I spotted his car in the parking lot.) "He's with a client, you say? Well, I am just going to leave this envelope here for the contribution that he generously promised last month." Pause, she reluctantly takes it. "And of course, if it would be easier for him, I could come by pick the checkup." I will relay that to Mr. Padilla, thanks.

We were doing the state a favor by our very existence, as I saw it. Reclaiming a parolee from the ultimate secret society with its ingrained codes that go back to childhood is no small task.

2

The parallels to school and this place are unavoidable, as I sit here on my favorite bench: the affirming recognitions, the hollow pleasantries, the shared burden of required attendance. Actually, more than that, as the complexities wait outside the shiny floors of this building as well. We are scheduled midway down the agenda today, what with two days of carryovers. My attitude is not good today, which is why I have found a seat a long way down this bench. I struggle with protocol, no matter how I might pretend otherwise. I rehearse in my mind what is to come. "Mr. Chairman" [eye contact], "members of the committee" [look them over]. Then my remarks—succinct and to the point. Turn it over swiftly to our Hope House resident, always the most effective way of presenting our program.

And what am I supposed to do when the creepy Senator from the West Side does his *thing?* Tall, the way he lurks in a bar, always alone—the way his booming voice carries across any room with its cloddish import. But then, he has a very specific relationship with Jesus, as I caught him explaining one night on late TV, the local evangelical channel. I do channel surf. "As you know, Gary," he said to the late-night host, "we in government have lost our moral way. We have taken God out of the legislative process. At our own loss, of course." At this point I was trying to remember in what drunken condition I had spotted him last, moving from bar to bar in the State Capitol, on the prowl. But I will try to be respectful when he cues himself and asks a question about incarceration that will prove that he is informed about our presence. I must have a high tolerance for the inauthentic and this fine winking; in fact, I am sure that I do it well enough. Plus, I owe it to my organization, my employer, to be respectful to the Senator. We are in trouble, financially. We need the money to stay open, this state appropriation with an emergency clause for extra credit. Besides, I do not do conflict well. I actually *like* the guy on some level. Or he's sympathetic, the way Nixon was, in all of his oddity—these oafish fathers who have done their wounding.

But I wanted to be up here, full-time, in his and my opponent's place. Right now, I am waiting for the legislators to cease their long-talking formality, so that they can adjourn to committees and we can get traction on moving our respective bills forward. At least I am alone this afternoon. The usual, to-be-expected interruptions, certain lobbyists quick to point out that we are *not* in the budget, *not* where we should be—Senate Bill whatever—or well-meaning friends checking on my condition. What, because I lost an election, I am supposed to be all emotionally fragile? Like I'm in need of surveillance?

And speaking of emotional fragility, I suppose I should get into what became of Kit and me. It's just hard … all of that time—*years*—all of that effort. The short summary is that after the euphoria of me returning from the freight trains, and both of us committing to our life together, the same patterns began to assert themselves. Inevitably. The thing about being in your early thirties is that other lives, other choices dance on your periphery, haunt you even as maybe your chosen pairing does not feel as it should. The promise, the adventure in an enticing stranger. I am sure Kit felt the same kind of pull to explore outside our hardwood-floored haven. Our arguments took the same shape as before our reconciliation: my work, always my *work*. And her lack of confidence in her artwork. It is not like we grew to hate each other. We had way too much in common to go down that route. This commonality, this deep understanding of each other, was the foundation of our relationship. The problem was it only went so far. There were too many energies pulling us apart, both inside and outside our house.

And then there was her illness, which put a strain on our dynamic. I was not about to abandon her on that front, and it was further complicated as the doctors and alternative practitioners could never figure out what was wrong with her. But the symptoms were real enough: fatigue, lack of balance, dizziness, chronic pain. Kit is not one to complain, and she would go about her life as best she could—working in her studio, making dinner for us both, walking the dogs. But her health limitations began to affect our relationship, in obvious and not-so-obvious ways. Increasingly, she was not up for going out to a restaurant, or to a friend's party, which only encouraged my life outside our relationship to take root and flourish. Since becoming an adult, I have always needed to have different worlds in play. But the key for me is to keep my moral balance, to become consciously schizophrenic, to be on top of these different worlds. In control.

I can see in retrospect that I was not being honest with myself or Kit at the time, that I was in fact checking out of our pact, however unintentionally. She needed more from me. She always needed more from me, but she had too much pride to force the issue, to actually ask me specifically for what she needed. Again, her illness did not help, making her increasingly dependent upon others, upon me. She quietly checked out of our relationship as well (of course I can see this all in retrospect). The exit came in the form of her suddenly re-emergent sister, who lived back East, who was willing to fully commit to the uncertainty of her illness. Such a third party made it easier on us both, softened the whole process of selling our house and dividing up the furniture, with Kit keeping the dogs, naturally. And maybe someday we could resume our inescapable life bond?

Shortly after returning from my freight-train-induced soul quest, I became a single man again. A bachelor. But that proved to be short-lived, which I will go into later.

3

It was awkward at first, this running for public office. I really did not know what to expect, but the challenges it presented became apparent soon enough. Sisto down at the clerk's office watched my learning curve with amusement, but he did help me out in the process.

"Fella," he said one day, "as you know, you are entitled to challenge your opponent's signatures. But the deadline is coming up soon."

"This is news to me," I replied.

"I shouldn't say this," he continued, "as we are supposed to be neutral, but I did notice that she did not bring in a whole lot of signatures. They are probably pretty confident about her winning again. And maybe they know that you don't know much about how to go about this." Sisto smiled. "Just kidding, of course."

"No offense taken," I said.

I dimly remembered how many signatures I was required to bring in, but others had told me to double that number, and I had done that. I asked Sisto how I would go about checking her signatures.

"I have them right here," he said, flashing that smile that I had increasingly come to appreciate." But you are on your own now."

"Much appreciated," I said. And then I had no clue what to do next.

Senator Cohen, the sponsor of our Hope House legislation, proved helpful in these circumstances, but I did try to limit my questions. In this case, she pointed out that the trial lawyers were our natural allies, as Democrats, and that they usually handled the business of challenging signatures. The problem in my case, though, she gently pointed out, lay in the fact that my prospects for winning the race seemed remote at best. To them at least. Obviously, I was not an incumbent. Why would they take the time and energy to go through each signature, as they would routinely do for her if she had a challenger? I was on my own, which was fine with me, actually. It all seemed rather petty to me, bad form even. A race should be won or lost fair and square, not decided upon some technicality, and it looked like she had enough signatures to me on the nominating petitions in the envelope that Sisto had provided. I was hardly in the position to go through some court proceeding on this front.

Other more substantial fronts awaited me, as it would turn out.

One thing that became immediately accessible to me, however, was the wisdom of going door to door. It was the tradition in my newly claimed home, voters expected as much—especially from a challenger—and I soon realized that this was something that I enjoyed. Or mostly enjoyed. It was not difficult to obtain walk lists from the party (Sisto had his limitations with what he could do on my behalf) and good precinct maps, so off to the streets and gravel roads I went. I had had an initial taste of this process when I obtained the signatures to be the official Democrat nominee in Senate District 10. It seemed fairly simple to me: knock on the door of a Democratic household, explain who I was, invoke party loyalty, and ask if they would sign my ballot petition. Being new to the neighborhood, to the district, to the process, I did get questions. Such as, "Who are you again?" And, "I have never seen you around here before." I then explained that I had grown up in Iowa but had *chosen* to live here because New Mexico was such an amazing place. And friendly too. Yes, I had moved into an older Hispanic neighborhood, and I was clearly not Hispanic. Had no family in the district. But ultimately it was enough to be a *Democrat* (my new official party). And everyone seemed to have an Irish uncle or cousin, which did not hurt my case either.

In terms of searching for omens, for proof that this was the right direction for me, as a neophyte candidate canvassing in neighborhoods that were foreign to me, it was my second week when I knocked on Charlie Brophy's door. A silver-haired man with bright blue eyes—clearly Irish—he looked me over thoroughly before responding to my front door pitch. "We need to talk," he finally said. And not feeling the agency to decline, I accepted his invitation to join him on his patio for a beer.

"You are new at this, aren't you?" he asked, handing me the beverage in a frosted glass.

"How did you guess?" I replied, not taking offense.

"It was in the way you introduced yourself. Too tentative, too apologetic. Plus, I have never heard of you. I have been active in Democratic politics here in District 10 for years."

"A person has to start with this somewhere, right?" I answered. He had a gentle manner.

"Who are you again?"

"Chapman Murphy. Democratic candidate for Senate District 10."

"You know that you have the wrong last name for this kind of thing?"

"I have been told that." I remembered Sisto's comments to that effect.

"Don't get me wrong," Charlie continued. "We have had some great Anglo representatives in this district over the years. Do you remember Nathan Kelsey?"

I shook my head. "I am still sort of new to the state."

"Well, he almost won the Governor's race. Should have, really. And he started just like you, going door to door. He was a State Rep for at least a decade, I can't remember how long."

"That's good to know, "I replied. "What kind of beer is this, anyway? It's really good. "

"St. Pauli Girl. I keep it on tap. I should serve you Harp or Guinness or something like that, but I prefer the German beers. So why should I support your candidacy?"

"Umm … well, I am a Democrat, for starters."

"And you are it, right? No primary involved?"

"Correct."

"So, you have a pulse. And you are in my party. Why else?"

"I want to make New Mexico a better place."

"Indeed. That's admirable. Why else?"

"I just think we can do better. We don't have to be 49th in everything. Which we seem to be."

"You *are* new here," Mr. Brophy teased. "Clearly."

"Is that such a bad aspiration?" I replied defensively.

"No, but it's way too general. People want specific reasons to vote for you. Especially if you hope to get crossover votes, which you need in this district to win. Which is why you didn't have a primary."

"The Bluffs?"

"Yes, the Bluffs," he sighed. "But not just up there. The district has changed since Kelsey had it. Damned re-districting. We got screwed."

"I have been told that."

"What do you do for a living?" he continued.

"I work with ex-convicts."

"Oh, great."

"No, seriously," I replied. "Have you heard of Hope House?"

He shook his head.

"It's a well-regarded residential program for parolees, men and women. We try to reclaim individuals from the criminal justice system."

"Okay," he said. "That sounds noble. Do you have any specific issue that is propelling this run of yours? Beyond wanting to make New Mexico a better place?"

I thought for a moment. "I am still kind of working on my platform."

"That's fine. Actually, most people won't care what you stand for. They will judge you fairly quickly when they open their door. It doesn't help that you are new here. You are from … where? The Midwest?"

"Iowa."

"Right. Well, we all come from someplace else. Except our Native American brothers and sisters, of course."

Despite the sobering direction of our conversation, the beer was tasting really good in the hot May afternoon. And I felt that Mr. Brophy was trying to help me. Plus, I could tell that he knew what he was talking about.

"Well," I began, "do you have any suggestions?"

"Start raising money."

"I supposedly do that for a living. With Hope House, I mean. I should be able to pull that off."

"How much do you have right now?"

"Not much," I said, with honesty.

"That has to change. Immediately. Hit up your friends. And your family even. You need money to get your message out. "

"Which I am still working on."

"That's fine. You have time. But the money needs to happen now. There are groups for us like the unions and trial lawyers that will help. They need to be convinced, though, that you have a chance of winning. The common wisdom is that District 10 is out of reach. People like the incumbent. They respect her. How long has she been there?"

"I'm not sure."

"You need to know that. You need to research her votes to see if she has any that could make her vulnerable. Do you have anybody helping you?"

"Not really."

"Well, that needs to change as well. There are some good campaign managers out there for us. But that costs money too. You will need a good one."

"Okay."

"Listen," he said, draining his glass. "Did you want another beer?"

"No," I answered, feeling slightly buzzed. "I need to get back out there. On your street."

"That you can do. And you are smart to start like this. It doesn't cost anything, and people will remember that you visited their house."

"The incumbent, she doesn't walk the neighborhoods."

"She's a Republican. She doesn't have to."

"Listen," he repeated, "I like you. You have got a good presence about you. You just need work. Let me walk you out."

I gathered my clipboard and my stapled walk-lists and followed him to the door.

"Here is something that should help," he said, shaking my hand one last time with a folded check in his palm. "I can help you later too. And get some signs printed up that you can put in yards like mine."

"Okay," I said, truly surprised and flattered.

"But make sure that they are union signs. That they have the union bug on them. It matters to our side. To our people."
I turned and faced him, shaking his hand firmly. "Thank you *so much.*"

"You can best thank me by winning. Now go hit those doors."

It took me a couple of days to process this visitation from Charlie Brophy. I was increasingly aware of how much work awaited me, and it was daunting not knowing exactly where to begin. But it was affirming to know that walking the district was a good thing, and I was definitely in the groove on that front. These lists were good. And people were very friendly, for the most part.

4

At least I am not having those dreams anymore, the ones where I am running my fingers through my opponent's hair. (It *was* distracting during the debates, how jet black and thick her hair was, inviting something in that regard, but I kept my focus—anyone who was there will tell you.) Or the dream where I have three days in which to recruit an additional forty volunteers—personally—with our own attack piece yet to hit. Things might seem a little flat on this government bench right now, but at least my sleep is returning. We should probably hope for yet another continuance, as we could probably get Cesare, our ace witness, up here tomorrow to testify. Always better that way, rather than just the well-intentioned droning of the officeholders.

Her hair was, and is, definitely jet black, and the local paper loved her—not that it would have made any difference. Whatever transpired several months ago, back in November, many of us are trying to sort out—intellectually, morally, emotionally. My deal is kind of simple, though—I had an opportunity to win if perhaps a different nominee was up there at the top, on the presidential level. At least my campaign debt is relatively modest. I just felt some need *deep within* to run against her—nothing personal—just wanted the other side of that line, and the red license plate with all of the affirmation it would bring.

"If you told me that you were going to run against me," she whispered tensely that night at the candidate forum, "then I would not have supported Hope House like I did. Last session."

I never understood what she was worried about anyway, especially as the campaign progressed—she had the numbers, the new Republican homes springing up everywhere in the district, the impressive résumé, and a hometown success story no less. Who was I anyway? Just some Anglo guy from out of state nervous enough to knock on all of those doors: entire blocks, neighborhoods, precincts … I thought I could outwork her—and did, seeing as how she did virtually nothing—which made her victory potentially more humiliating.

"You did well, fella." It was another lobbyist guy.

"Hey, Vazquez," I replied, getting up from the bench. "Good to see you."

"She's a tough one to beat." He always looked elegant, with his neatly trimmed moustache and tailored suits. "Plus, what they did to the district."

"Well, thanks for your help. You voted for me, right?"

"Sure, I did. Made sure my kids did, too."

"Thanks, guy … How's the session going?"

"Busy. All of these bills …. You gonna do it again?"

"Oh, I don't know about that. But I'm gonna remain active."

"Sorry I couldn't do more. But like I told you, she has been good to my clients. My tribe supports incumbents."

"I understand. Money wasn't really the issue."

"Maybe I can help you more next time."

"That's okay."

"Why don't you cross over?" he asked with a grin. "You kind of look like a Republican."

"No way, man. That ship has sailed."

Which is not entirely true, of course. I get the other side loud and clear, growing up as I did in my own family. The bootstraps worldview, how irritating government can be, how malingerers take advantage, how beautiful the free market is, et cetera. Whenever I am in their company— brothers, dad, numerous jock friends quick with their cynical comments—it is invariably unsettling because it speaks clearly to me. Deep down. It is what I, too, was taught: we smile in recognition and inevitably ridicule the government, bureaucracy the big cartoon. It is more personal than this, really: we are not *insensitive* to the suffering around us—the welfare office, the missing fathers, the gangs, the botched aspiration—we want a better world, too. But you cannot legislate fairness, our darker instincts will always be with us, blah blah blah.

"Chapman Murphy, Chapman Murphy," my name over the loudspeaker. "Please go to room 311."

"Okay, then," I said to myself, gathering up my belongings. "Down the hall we go."

Just because I went to an Ivy League school does not mean that my vocational place in the world should not be selling raffle tickets every weekend in the churches, or in front of a supermarket, or a WalMart. It is something that I know that my father did his best to understand when he was alive, but there was not a lot of progress on his end. I would have reminded him, if the opportunity had arisen, that we Irish are not that far removed from our carnival-inclined ancestors—no matter how *Americanized* we have become. Or at least that has been the case with me. But I was always the odd one in the family. How could I explain to Dad the deep satisfaction in stuffing our cash in our sleeved bank envelopes—in fives and tens—all going directly to our monthly operational expense, which was always iffy on the revenue side? His world was framed by corporate reports, trustee meetings, conferences on business development, not by a New Mexico parking lot in late July, mid-afternoon sun—at least not bad on the humidity front—me and my colorful parolees, selling our tickets, their tattoos and inappropriate outfits. Too much skin.

And then the beauty in our annual holiday dinner—held strangely at the local country club or high-end restaurant. Targeting the legal donor community, bestowing the inevitable award on one of our attorney supporters, and featuring of course the emotional testimony by one of our residents. We established our place on the local charitable calendar—the first Saturday night in December—and I would go about the business of lining up our array of silent auction items (no comment here), and of course the relentless logistics of cost per meal, rental of the space, the *program*. Not cheap, our Hope House Holiday Dinner, and it pained me personally to issue that check, wanting always a significant profit on the whole thing. That I could report to my board, and of course more specifically to our new

Finance Committee. But there was that one year, that one December, when one of my favorite donors, the patriarch of a successful local Irish Catholic family—mostly but not exclusively active in the law—wanted to see the bill. He pulled me aside quietly, as was his way, politely after most of the attendees had left, the wait service staff breaking down the tables and chairs:

"Young man," Mr. O'Connor said, with his gentle cadence. A tall man, who always reminded me of Atticus Finch. "May I see the bill? I am just curious what a fine event like this actually costs."

"By all means, sir," my ready reply. I handed him the yellow receipt.

"I was very impressed with your speaker this year. What was his name again?"

"Reggie. He's done well in our program."

"I can see that. His story was quite moving."

"We are certainly hopeful about his future," I replied. "I used to do all of the intake interviews, at the prisons across the state. I learned in my first month that we just can never predict how one of our residents will fare."

"It's God's work," Mr. O'Connor stated bluntly. "How can we humans know?"

"No argument there," I answered, feeling always at these moments like a bit of an impostor. "How was your steak, by the way?"

"Excellent, as usual," he replied. "You know that I belong to this Country Club?"

"Yes, I knew that. We needed someone to vouch for us … and you were that person."

"I belong mainly for business purposes, of course. And when my children were younger, they liked to play tennis."

"It's a nice setup here."

"I am not much on golf. But I hear it is an excellent course."

"I have heard that as well."

"Well, Chapman, I have enjoyed our conversations in my office."

"I have too, sir."

"Did you know that I once thought about the priesthood?"

"It doesn't surprise me, I confess. Just based on what we usually end up talking about. Spiritual matters and such."

"What is the point of all this," he continued, addressing both our immediate surroundings and of course a more important, larger context, "if we who have been blessed do not give back?"

"I hear you, sir."

He paused. He looked at the bill. "I've got this. Don't worry about it this year."

"What?" I interjected. "You mean you want to pay for all of this? Dinner for 300 people?"

He nodded. "It was an excellent event. I go to a lot of these, you know. And that Reggie…."

"Are you sure, Mr. O'Connor?"

He pulled out his checkbook. "Who do I make it out to? Hope House? Or the Club?"

"Uh, sir, I am speechless. I guess to the Club. That would be simpler. You can claim it on your taxes, right?"

"That's not important," he replied, in his characteristically soft tone. "Your work is what matters."

"I will never forget this, Mr. O'Connor." I hugged him. I wiped off tears with my hand. I tried not to think about what I could report to my Finance Committee.

"You just keep doing this work," he answered. "Somebody has to."

5

I don't know why I ever thought that I could make it in, cross the line; the people here in the hallway—the legislators—they are a conventional sort. And I am not the only one in these hallways who has tried—it's that dividing line I have been up against my entire life, deep down, where no one can see it. The part of me that is *actually here* needs to be bolstered by something else. I have it in my mind that if I were elected, it would change everything. My issues would not be so glaring, I could have an undeniable place in the world, symbolized of course by my special red license plate. But honestly, I don't know if I could ever really fit in here. Others up here pull it off, in their pantsuits, or the men walking in the importance of the role thrust upon them. I can wear a suit, easily enough—I like suits—but how strange it would be to be *in* the club, behind the microphone, an unapologetic participant in the weight of literal, public office.

One more thought on the triumph of that holiday fund-raising dinner: as it happened, Reggie relapsed less than a week afterwards—he just vanished, as our residents do, until parole picked him up at a motel on the drug avenue. It did occur to me, and I shared this with my Finance Committee, we should be more careful in who we elevate as our holiday speaker; the same thing that happened with Reggie has happened with others. Something about the euphoria of a respectful if not adoring dinner audiences—judges in the room as well—might trigger the impulse to celebrate. Or to calm down. Reggie stole some money from where he was employed, which complicated things, as it would represent a new felony, not just a parole violation.

These were my people.

"Senator Murphy!" It was Carlos, yet another of my favorite gentlemen of the hallways.

"Not even, buddy," I replied. "I lost."

"Ah, but you did good."

"It wasn't *that* close. But thanks for the help—I'll miss our little dance."

"Dance? What dance?" Carlos asked. He was wearing his fedora. Bushy black moustache, like a certain Iraqi dictator.

"You *know,*" I said teasingly. "Under the table?" I rubbed my fingers.

"Oh, that?" he replied, laughing. "Where are you from again?"

"Not here."

"Seriously? I would not have known that." He was always good with the deadpan.

"You reported that, right?"

"Did *you?*" he fired back, perhaps teasing. Never sure with Carlos.

"Well," I began, "there is that anonymous category. For anonymous cash under the table. But you reach the limit pretty quick. What is it, three hundred?"

"I don't know that stuff," Carlos replied, ready to change the subject.

"You've got a bunch of clients this session, don't you?"

"I do okay," he said, shrugging his shoulders.

"Okay? You're the man. Are you doing both the pit-bull breeders and the humane society again? Or whatever they're called?"

"Certain interests need to be represented."

"You're all right. I know you care, which sets you apart."

"It's a living, man."

"It's a good one. Besides, ever since my desert island dream … you had my back in that one, buddy."

"How did that go again?" Carlos asked, trying to remember.

"Oh, just the usual. I'm alone on this island, see? And I'm trembling, kind of freaked out. It's like I've isolated myself, even on this freakin' desert island. But then *you* appear, put your hand on my shoulder, and say: 'Don't worry. It's okay to have done this to yourself. It's not unprecedented,' you say."

"Were there women on this island?"

"I *told* you, that was later in the dream. The point was, that even a relatively macho guy like yourself could relate to the feeling in the dream."

"I'm not macho. I'm sensitive."

"I know. Like in the dream."

"Was Mrs. Howell in the dream?"

"Shut *up*."

"Weren't you just paged now?"

"Hey, you noticed!" I exclaimed. "In between your deals."

"It's early. Even for a short session. *Temprano*."

I went off in search of Room 311, which should not have been *that* hard to find. Definitely not like old times, when I would literally be running—or at least very nervous—as the fate of our legislation, which had never made it before, seemed to hang daily on the posted committee agendas and the hidden code of the entire place. A few more polite hellos and the room was located: House Finance. It was Mike.

6

You had to like a smile like his—that wry grin—gray hair, intelligent, in shape, and very right wing.

"Did you page me, Mike?"

"None other."

"What on earth for?"

"Well, I am not totally in the service of what you would call the dark side."

"No, we understand each other. Though you know you're in the wrong camp."

"Not me, buddy. You're talking about yourself."

"Nope. It's just where I *am*."

"We had a seat for you. You could have won that one—no problem. Played in the *game*."

"No, don't rub it in. The *game*?"

"Yes. Where with your jump shot, I think you could score at least twenty points."

"Please."

"You'd have a uniform and everything."

"You know me too well. The two reasons why I ran."

"See?"

"The only problem is, I am *not* a Republican."

"If you say so."

"Anyway, we have legislation this session. You know our financial situation. The board has met, right?"

"That's why I called you in here. Anything I can do?'"

"Just help me with your Republican colleagues."

"Done."

"It's dire. We have operational funds for about one month. We are changing lives and such."

"Can you get your residents up here?"

"For sure. Travel passes from parole. Et cetera." I paused for a second, wanting to change the subject. "You might have us on the national front. But this is still a Blue State."

"Not this election."

"This one doesn't count. We are in charge here. God help us."

"You have that right."

"How are things going for you?" I asked.

Mike paused, grew pensive. I noticed that he had not shaved, which was quite unusual for the top corporate attorney at our state's largest law firm. "I am frustrated. But it's still early."

"What, they are not letting you close to the fire? Upstairs?"

"They won't let me near that sword. I just want to hack away a bit."

"Sure. *A bit.*"

"Government cannot solve these problems. You know that. Your dad taught you—"

"It's not that simple."

"And this Governor? Jesus."

"Well, you had that sword, you fellas, for what, the last eight years? It's only fitting, our turn."

"We'll get it back. Though I wish you would have won your race." Mike smiled. "Don't tell anyone. We could use your jump shot up here."

"I was cursing your name this past summer."

"I only told you what should have been obvious."

"But I *did* have a chance."

"Not with the way the district is. Now."

"Touché. Those new houses—that Republican planet that just sort of sprang up? I didn't know it even existed. It wasn't on my maps or anything. It was the Sunday after we spoke, after you told me I had no chance. All of those streets named after Mediterranean trees. I thought, 'damn that Mike. Bastard. There are no Democrats here.'"

"That was the intention. I drew the map."

"Bastard."

"You gave it a good shot. You had us worried. Sort of."

"Well, you must have been worried. You went negative."

Mike laughed. "Only after you called her a liar."

"I didn't do that. That was the party."

"Did she go negative?"

"Yeah. She called me an idiot."

"So, it was the idiot versus the liar?"

"More or less. I didn't take it personally—in fact, if that's as bad as it gets … I didn't have any bench warrants or anything out there like that. … Did I?"

"I don't know. Do you?"

"*No*. I'm just saying … I kept waiting for the *big* hit piece. You're checking the mailbox for your own public humiliation. And then, when it came, it was just not that big of a deal. Just some grainy photo of me as grainy boy, and lots of references to ex-felons. And these things that I presumably said at one of our debates, taken completely out of context."

"You ran a good race. The numbers are the numbers."

"I know."

"Now what?"

"Fuck, I don't know. I'm all jammed up. I can't move again. Hard enough fighting that label. Carpetbagger."

"Why not?"

"Democrats don't do that. That's what you people do."

"You people?"

"Look, all I know is that the right way is rarely the easy way, and all of that."

"I still think you're one of us."

"No way. By birth only."

"Those are strong ties."

"Yeah, until you get into the specifics of the *present tense.*"

"How's your shot?"

"I suck. You?"

"We are getting older, buddy."

"No way."

"Just let me know if I can help."

"You're all right, guy."

I have a lot of friendships like that up here—it's kind of a character flaw, to be forgiving just because a guy like that compliments me on my jump shot and recognizes my upbringing, which is supposed to be a big secret and all. His politics are mean and self-concerned. And what an ass he was that night: "You have no chance," he told me, in between drinks, eyes narrowed. "Unless your Governor gives you a hundred thousand dollars. And even if he does …." And then, that following Sunday afternoon, staring up at the hot, lonely street of new Southwestern houses, searching for Democratic or even Independent households. Rows upon rows of freshly built enemies, though I did try to make my case. Especially so, with this unsettling new neighborhood: face-to-face, follow-up notes, minimizing the reality of our divided nation. The people were very nice— they smiled, accepted the campaign flier with my fluorescent white teeth, and thanked me for coming by. Didn't matter— I got slaughtered in that precinct, though not as badly as the guy at the top of the ticket, who apparently the nation did not care for. Was it his brief flirtation with a fake British accent? Or those dated yet effective film clips? Or the relentless testimonials of the embittered veterans?

Anyway, I remember that day as well as any day during the five-month campaign. It's just embarrassing to have worked that hard, to have walked the way I did. Every night, every weekend, a kind of obsession, and completely obvious in its need. And my opponent, not doing a whole lot, really. Rumors of her ambivalence—a victory for me and my life would somehow be validated, the lost decades and less-than-ideal choices would be transformed. But that particular Sunday afternoon, hot in August, staring at limitless Olive Street or whatever it was called, Mike's prediction made my optimism turn. Bastard. I was on the wrong side of that winner/loser line once again. Our nation's president had his yard signs at every other house in this neighborhood. Shit. And yet there's something deep within that just refuses to quit, that leads me to redouble the doomed effort, just on the outside chance—it's being an outside chance the whole reason to choose it.

And then there was my girlfriend in open rebellion at just how much time this takes, not understanding how intense my need for approval was. Emily. More on her, on us, later. Coming home at night exhausted, unable to talk with her on the phone—and the tension *that* created. And then the gradual emergence of the better reasons for the whole exercise, nearly every day a conversion experience of a sort—how important this is, people's lives and what they want for their kids, and the fear everywhere to be calmly approached, the attempt at reassurance if given an opening. To a household, the longing for something better than what is, and with each passing day I wanted even more to be their State Senator. For the better reasons of empathy and service (not the license plate and the game). But everything can be simplified or reduced into a formula and lost decades and late starts do have their impact. What if the business about the freight trains became common knowledge, for example? Or the bench warrants that I am sure to have floating around somewhere, maybe even buried in my glove compartment?

"Hey, Murphy!" It was Joshua, a young political operative.

"God—is everyone up here or what? Doesn't anybody have a life?"

"What's that supposed to mean?" Hair slicked back, cowboy boots.

"Oh, just the ravings of a defeated candidate."

"Now, the key for you now is to be *seasoned*. Not *beaten.*"

"I know. It's all about the messaging."

"What else is there? Truly?"

"If you say so."

"You should get married," Joshua continued, after sizing me up like a prized calf. "It would help you."

"Are you serious?"

"You're still with that Emily, right?"

"Right."

"It's working? It's been a couple of years, right?"

"Sort of. But you're putting it all in this political context."

"You don't need a cloud like that. However old you are—"

"I'm *old.*"

"And still unmarried? What's up with that?"

"It's called being a bachelor."

"You know what I mean."

"I thought they might do something like that in the campaign. But they didn't"

"They didn't have to."

"You're saying that I should run again? That it's winnable?"

"I'm saying that there are voters in that district that you connect with. You've proven it."

"I was just talking with Mike Powell."

"He's a dick."

"So are you."

"Okay, what did *Mike Powell* say?"

"What you would expect—that the district is out of reach now."

"Look, it's just in how you present yourself."

"The messaging, right?"

"That's what I mean. You don't care about a whole lot of things, do you?"

"Well, I care about what I *care about*. But like with motorcycle helmets. People shouldn't be forced to wear them if they don't want to."

"Exactly."

"And pit bulls. We should not mess with people's dogs. It's like an indigenous tradition out here. And I'm from freakin' Iowa or wherever."

"Correct. You are a 'pragmatic progressive.' An exception to the NPR crowd."

"My brother was a logger. I mean, for a of couple of years at least. After he graduated from Yale."

"That's what I mean."

"And my dad went to school with half of this president's cabinet members, I mean the old ones. Back East, where *you're* from."

"I'm from here."

"Okay, I stand corrected. How do you function in that office of yours? It's depressing."

"You mean at the strip mall?"

"Yeah, like you could be in D.C. Running somebody's campaign or working on The Hill."

"We were talking about *you.*"

"But you have that killer instinct—I don't have it. I will be honest with you. I just don't care in that kind of way. I'm not really *here.*"

Joshua paused. "We'll work on that."

"How are things at The Party?" I asked.

"They suck. We've got a lot of ground to make up."

"Well, I'm not *moving to the center.*"

"You don't have to. You're already there."

"I just don't like being trapped in these labels."

"But look at you. You do God's Work."

"It's a job. It's called the nonprofit sector."

"But with the ex-convicts?"

"Parolees. It's a better term."

"Fine. It's a Biblical calling."

"For some people it is."

"The least of our brothers and sisters?"

"Don't joke around about that. It's true."

"You came to our state to do God's Work."

"*Please.*"

Joshua shifted his attention to my work area on the bench. "What the fuck is that?" he asked, nodding towards the variety of business cards splayed out on my Capitol seat. Different colors, rubber bands, wrinkled shards of paper.

"That," I answered, "is my filing system."

"Dude. People talk about stuff like that."

"Let them. I text on my cell phone, don't I?"

"How old *are* you?"

"You don't wanna know."

"Anyway, you look beaten, dude."

"I was beaten. I am beaten." Joshua was silent. "Okay, I am not beaten. I'm seasoned."

"That's better. And do something about all of those cards."

"Look, I even have a website, okay? Don't give me a hard time."

"Let's have lunch," he replied, "after the session."

"Deal," I answered.

And off Joshua went, with the purpose of the young.

I have to admit, some of the reasons for my State Senate run were less than pure. I really did want that red license plate. And the *game* ... I could not resist fantasizing about how many points I could score. The Annual House Vs. Senate charity game, everyone in newly minted uniforms representing the two major universities in our state—cheerleaders, bands, mascots—all in attendance, the gym nearly packed. The only way you could be on the team was to be elected. No young staffers, advocates, lobbyists allowed. The older legislators would stumble around, their faces disturbingly red, and the younger guys were hardly impressive as well. But full refereed quarters, the final score barely reaching twenty points on each side.

And then there was just my general, overall irreverent nature. The whole political process felt like high school—in its predictability, its obviousness, its inevitable choosing of sides—so why not approach it like performance art? Satirize the experience while fully participating in it. Instead of the solemn campaign slogan that was forced upon me—*the path to a brighter future*—how about, *more than a local curiosity, Murphy will surprise you.* Something like that. And campaign fliers with a photo of a doughnut hole with the candidate sticking his middle finger through it. Something non-linear and non-sensical. Or on the back of said flier testimonials like, "*Chapman Murphy saved my life. No, really, he did.*" Or, "*Murphy was voted best-dressed boy in the seventh grade.*" Or, "*Not only is he a licensed driver, but he has a checking account as well.*" The possibilities were endless.

But I was in this game, for sure, and as the months progressed, the more serious it became.

7

I am an unusual fellow—people will tell you that. Running for political office can really shake things loose, the naked public invitation of it all. For example, it is approaching March and I still have my Christmas tree up—needles brittle and brown and ready to be ignited by my string of hot colored lights. Or the spectacle of my car, the way my whole work life is buried in layers on top of the back seat, discarded plastic bottles everywhere, the empty cappuccino cups piled high. The facts that my *important* papers are there on the dashboard, in the reserved left front area, and that months have gone by and I have yet to change my expired plates testify to some unknown logic. My insurance lapsed way back when. On the home front, I can periodically summon the motivation to clean the dishes piled high in the sink— some accomplishment considering that I never eat at home—and of course I do have every intention of cleaning up my front entrance or yard or whatever it is called. This is quite a contrast from my days with Kit, part of my bachelor identity, no doubt. The hose is an entangled mess and has assumed the permanence of a frozen sculpture, and I have had to step over it for quite some time now. And the yucca bush is definitely dead.

I wonder if these neighbors of mine voted for me. Did I carry the compound in spite of my obvious issues? The election was crazy. It was all could do to stay up with what they needed me to do immediately. Or by the end of tomorrow. My professional campaign team. Questionnaires from the horseback riding association, the meeting with the plumbers and pipefitters, the planned weekend "Murphy for a Brighter Tomorrow" group canvass and wondering just how many of my recruits would actually show. And those goddamned debates.

"Chapman," he had called me, my campaign manager, characteristically urgent. "You need to answer your phone. We need to make a decision. You need to call me back *immediately*."

Emily, the new woman in my life, understands. Plus, she has her painting and all of that—why am I always drawn to artistic women? As long as I can call Emily every night and not succumb to the temptation of leaving her messages. There is the bashed-in bathroom door that I will not go into. You can imagine that I do not entertain much—especially for a political candidate—as there would be too much explaining to do.

But I know I should at least visit with Manuel and Rosalita and all of the very nice people who voted for me. And I really do want to go to Mass down the street, where I will see all of them. This fantastic old neighborhood, Spanish families going back centuries, everyone very nice to me, the energetic one from Iowa. They are going to tease me, I know, about my truancy from their stunningly beautiful historic church, holy light streaming through stained-glass windows. "You just come here at election time," Manuel will say, grinning. "What kind of message is that to send to your constituents?" I will stutter an apology, loving him for all he did during those months. "I still have your signs," he will say, "if you want to come by and pick them up." I need Emily to do this with me. (I just need to make that 9:30 service.) Next week. And then Father Maestas, with how he chased off those messengers of extremity in the parking lot each weekend as the election neared (winking at me when no one was looking); those leaflets, with their disturbing imagery. Anyway, it would be enough just to show up. And my campaign team? I still owe them money, need to clear up that campaign debt. They tried hard on my behalf, and we were truly confident that I could pull off the upset. Our polling had me close. What a reckoning we all shared that evening.

9

"Chapman, are you ready to go on?" It was our sponsor, Senator Cohen.

"Sure," I replied. Her office was impressive: plaques acknowledging her decades of service, photos, numerous degrees under glass.

"Of course, I'm not sure we will *actually* be heard. We are still down a way on the agenda. Will it be just you?"

"It would work out fine if it took a while. We always like to have a resident speak—puts a face on it. Cesare has his travel pass and is on his way."

"Okay, that sounds good."

"Thanks, Margaret. I mean, Senator."

"Don't mention it. It's not a whole lot of money, and you're a great program. You do good work."

"How is your session going?" I asked her, surveying the many books just above her head.

"Oh, fine. I've got several bills that, well, stand a chance."

"That was very nice, by the way, what you said to me on election night. I mean, in front of the people with me—my campaign manager, my girlfriend, others."

"I meant it. If you can't win that seat, it can't be won."

"Again, that is very nice of you."

"Hey, Chapman!" It was Cesare, accompanied by our board president.

"Dude," I replied. "You're just in time. Thanks for bringing him up, Bob. I want you to meet our bill sponsor, Senator Margaret Cohen."

"Nice to meet you both," the Senator replied. They exchanged pleasantries. "I'm chairing another committee—but come and get me when you get close."

"Will do," I answered, as she exited her office. "Have any trouble finding this place?"

"No problem," Bob shrugged. "It's our State Capitol."

"You're looking sharp, Cesare." We were in the hallway now.

"Hey, anything for the cause, no?" He straightened his tie. "This is some place," he continued, wide-eyed and a little nervous. Yet another attractive staffer walked past, real nice cut of the skirt.

"Some change from prison, right?" I teased.

"Hey, any time you want me to come up here, *no problem*."

"It's a lot of waiting around. You both okay with that?"

"What's waiting?" Cesare answered. "I just did seven years."

"I'm retired," Bob added.

"This is great," I said. "The citizen legislature, in all of its ragged beauty."

"Who's ragged?" Cesare asked, uncertain.

"No, not that way."

"I'm ready," he replied. "This is important."

We actually did not have to wait long—a crowded room, it being early in the session and everyone on their best behavior. After retrieving Senator Cohen from her other important business, we were up. The microphone, the chair, the essential decorum.

"Mr. Chairman, members of the committee," I began, "I am here today with one of the current residents of our program. Cesare Morales is an example of the kind of client that we serve at Hope House. We're real proud of Cesare—he starts college in a month and he's working, what, two jobs now?"

"Three," Cesare clarified. "But they are all part time."

"Cesare, do you want to sit in that chair next to me and talk about why this program is so important?"

He made his way quickly through the aisle.

"Thank you," he said quietly into the microphone. "This is different than what I'm used to," he added, "I'm a little nervous." He looked around the important room. "All I know is, there's people like myself that want to change their lives. Inside the walls, I mean. For me, I was just tired of the gang life and, uh, being in trouble all the time. It's all I know. … I've hurt a lot of people close to me. My family … I want to make it up to them. I'm not thirty yet. I want to make something of my life."

Cesare stopped here, as emotion was starting to have its way. The usual committee room chatter died down.

"I'm sorry," Cesare continued. "It's just been a long road for me. But these people at Hope House, Mr. Murphy and others, they gave me a chance. Accepted me into their program. I have to pinch myself sometimes when I look at my life now. I have a checking account. ... And, uh, like Mr. Murphy said, I start school next month. *College.* They're helping me with all of this, and uh, I'm just not going back to the other life. No way."

"Mr. Chairman, members of the committee," I interjected, "I would just point out that Cesare is doing this *on his own*— in the sense that he is making these choices for himself. We are there to support him, that's all."

"I would like to add to these people," Cesare continued, "Mr. Chairman and all of that. You should fund this program. There are others like me who are waiting for a chance."

"Mister Chairman," Senator Cohen interrupted, "we will take questions now. If that would be appropriate?"

"Mr. Morales," a gray-haired, bespectacled man began, "I want you to know that we are very impressed with your testimonial. And this seems like a fine program, worthy of funding. I wish we had a Hope House in my district. I think we should just give them the money right now."

"We could use it right now," I could not resist saying. Laughter in the room. "In fact," I continued, "an emergency clause would be peachy."

"Senator Jones," Margaret began, "could not have said it any better. The taxpayer obviously wins out if someone doesn't re-offend. All the studies point to how ingrained the problem of recidivism is with this population. I would add, too, that they also accept women into their program, and they have a fine track record with their women's facility as well."

The thing about fund-raising is that it wears you down—year after year, the same dance with certain individuals and organizations, the thank you notes. I know that the charitable sector is supposed to serve the needs of the unserved, that government programs can only go so far, but what a burden on us all, the do-gooders! I am from a pragmatic world, if you are going to do something, you need to do it right. Solve homelessness. Neutralize criminal behavior. Make your city street safer. It just seems paltry, patchwork. Charity as an afterthought, or extra credit. A few random people are truly helped, big money and resources go elsewhere.

I suppose it is the thought that counts. Our donors and volunteers have always been a caring lot. Some were nervous making, like the guy with the mansion and the inclination to invite our younger male parolees over to show off his square footage. And his carpets going back to the time of Marie Antoinette, hung for full effect on the walls of his vaulted living room. He would come by the facility unannounced—helping out, sincerely—but he would zero in on a particular resident, often muscular, tattooed, young. He would purchase and donate expensive jewelry for my pivotal holiday dinner, raising our silent auction to a more credible level. I liked him, and he meant well. But as staff we would discuss our uneasiness, and one on one I would do likewise with certain members of my Finance Committee. Eventually he got the message and moved on to perhaps another worthy cause—something about his not being acknowledged for all he had done on behalf of Hope House. It was hard to stay up with the expectations of certain donors, and I suppose that has been my job, if I really cared about *that side* of my work. But I have not been keen on being the ultimate development professional, historically at least.

9

"I'm sorry I got all emotional," Cesare said, in the marble hallway outside the committee room.

"Dude, are you kidding?" I countered. "You were *great.*"
We had made a good impression, and I made sure to make the rounds with Cesare—introduced him to those who were randomly there (Attorney General, Carlos, Senate Leader, et cetera). Cesare was pumped up, feeling it as he looked at me with an animated expression. "This sure beats prison," he said to me again. "Or even Hope House—nothing personal. Did you see *her?*" he asked, a young man, handsome. Only one teardrop under his eye, the ink of initiation.

"Do you have a girlfriend?" I asked him, intent upon being a positive influence. "We have to stay focused here. Our program has no money."

"Yes, I have someone. But it's been tough. Being incarcerated and all. Do you?"

"Yes."

"What's her name?"

"Emily," I replied.

"How long you been going out?"

"A couple of years."

"Eeeh, no," Cesare laughed. "Decision time."

"It's a good relationship."

"Yeah, I have been working on that myself," Cesare replied. "I've always been a player. But with this one, we haven't even *slept* together yet." He laughed, flashing his white smile. "Back in the day, such a thing would be not even possible."

"It has more meaning that way, right?" I interjected. "Not that I've ever been much of a *player*."

"Sure," he winked. "If you say so."

"No, really. I always want something more. I get in these situations—"

"Yeah, I like not being in those situations all the time," he concurred, misunderstanding.

"Seven years?"

"Trafficking."

"State? Not Federal?"

"Yeah."

"I want your car, by the way." We were sitting on yet another Capitol bench. "Don't let me buy it from you," I continued. "What, that old thing?" Meaning his '77 Lincoln, with the lines and the tire holder.
"The interior, it just *gleams*. All white and shit." Inevitably, I succumbed to the lingo.

"It needs work."

"Did it really just sit all that time? What, on your family farm?"

"My uncle's place is kind of like that, on the outskirts. No, they just put it on blocks when I got sentenced."

"How come you didn't do Federal?"

"Because of the nature of the charges," he answered.

"The vinyl's peeling."

"It needs work."

"Good mileage?"

Cesare laughed. "Are you kidding? It costed me—seventy dollars? Last week, just going to work and back."

"What time does your shift start tonight?"

"Seven-thirty."

"We should get going," I said, getting off the bench. "Thanks again for doing this."

"Any time."

"It makes an impact. Otherwise it's just white guys like me droning on about a better world and shit."

"I can see you have a good life. I'd like something like that for myself—doing work that means something."
"Getting paid?"

"Yeah, that too." We were walking through the Rotunda. "I cannot believe what I was living."

"I imagine it has its allure."

"I suppose. It's just what I know."

"You've been through it. It carries weight—what you have to say."

"The straight life is fun, bro."

"It's pretty new, though, right? Maybe it's just the novelty of it all?"

"No. This is for reals."

"What are you going to major in?" Cesare looked at me, uncomprehending. "At school I mean?"

"Oh, uh, substance abuse counseling."

"Can I tell you something?"

"What do you mean?"

"My relationship. Emily gets jealous. It's a problem."

"I hate when that happens."

"I know our worlds are different, yours and mine. But I don't think she understands the concept of friendship. You know, between men and women. I have these relationships up here. But they are professional."

"Sure."
"No, for reals. But I am looking at it. I have to give Emily legitimate reasons."

Cesare thought for a moment. "We were talking at the house the other night about you—"

"I hate that shit."

"No, it was good. You're like a hustler. You're all street, whether you realize it or not."

"But I went to college. Back East even."

"That's cool. But you're still street. Like a hustler ... but for the good side."

"I'll take that as a compliment."

"You should."

I don't know what people actually say about me, but I *really* don't care to think about it. I don't know why I work with the ex-cons; my family was never enthused about it (especially my father, when he was alive). I suppose I am just a liberal arts casualty—courtesy of Brown University—but Wall Street or law school was just not my deal. All I know is that our ex-felons are invariably polite and respectful when I take them out on my fund-raising journeys—civic groups, churches, businesses. And they are similarly almost always received politely, if not warmly, by these same targets of our mission.

It was my night to cover dinner at the women's facility, which was a good thing because I had been meaning to check in on one of our fallen alumni. (Our residents are always falling, one way or another, as the term *recidivism* comes from the Latin *cadere,* meaning "to fall.") But Colter's case was different. I believe she is the only resident we allowed back into our program *three* times. Sadly, when our female parolees slip, they often end up out on Central Avenue, back in the life—the drugs, the motels, the seamy exchange of their bodies for money. I never actually saw Colter out on the avenue during her relapse, but I heard about it from the others. Thin, disoriented, from all reports. We thought she was gone.

But she came back. She cleaned herself up, reported to her parole officer, did a couple of weeks penance in the county jail, and now she was once again in our community.

"Chapman!" she exclaimed as I came through the front door.

"Colter," I replied. "You are back."

"Yes, I am, you crazy nut." We hugged each other.

"Are the volunteers here yet?" I asked.

"No. I think it's the group from Immanuel Lutheran." We looked at each other. "Yes, them," Colter continued, reading my thoughts.

"Okay."

"It's not polite to complain, Mr. Murphy. They are very well intentioned."

"I know, I know … I just cannot deal with that cole slaw they bring. And the casserole thing."

"Can we order Kentucky Fried after they leave?"

"You have my permission, as Development Director of Hope House."

Colter was already our house leader after only a few days of her resurrection. She had literally come back from the dead. The two of us went way back—I had done her first intake interview at the women's prison, back when I was actually running the program, and though small in number, we did have our successes (despite what you might hear to the contrary). Admittedly, I had no idea how to run a house full of earnest criminals trying to reform themselves; I can admit that I was not the strictest of disciplinarians *(rules? really?)*. But if probation and parole had their doubts about our program, in our early months of operation, at least our residents knew that we cared for them, to a person.

In Colter's case, due to what could be called her people skills, she was an easy choice to help with my relentless presentations, or anything else money related, which was truly my best role in this organization. I would pick her up on the weekends, or on weekdays after our programmatic dinner, and off we would go to tell our story. I came to know her particular story well over the succeeding months—which had to do with bad things in her childhood, a difficult father, and the inevitable sway of her similarly troubled classmates. She got married at seventeen, to an older man heavily into dealing meth, and had tremendous sadness about giving up her two boys.

When she fell, it had a certain impact on me at the time, apart from losing my ace ambassador. Our people, when they relapsed or went back, invariably did so in a quiet, off-site kind of way; their vanishing was usually dignified and ominous, and Colter's was no exception—the empty seat at our dinner table, our collective sinking feeling.

"I am back to stay now," she said, looking at me evenly. "I'm doing meetings. I *want* to do meetings. You have no idea what this last time was like."

"You were doing so well," I said, wanting to believe. "I mean—the therapy, the stuff around your lost kids ... sobriety."

"It was just too much," she said, starting to cry now. "I can't explain it. God works in strange ways."

"Apparently *He* does."

"I'm never going back, Chapman. This time it's for me."

"I believe you. Anyway, the only thing that matters is that you're here. You're back."

"You're damned right. Let's go sell some raffle tickets."

"Can I get you to say grace tonight? You know how I am about that."

"Of course."

One good thing about the non-profit world is the staffing that it attracts—young men and women who truly could be doing other things in business or international finance or law. Macey, our Executive Director, was fantastic, as Salazar had promised. Blonde hair, a master's degree in finance from some college back East—we hit it off immediately. Her husband was athletic, so I could not resist roping him into my local basketball culture. The roles were clear: Macey ran the program, presented to the full board every month, she wrote the grants, while I did my Murphy thing out in the community. Which involved my office off-site near the restaurants and coffee enclaves, and minimal meetings (except when I wanted to *sit in*). And I was welcome at the house, no more of *that* drama. I did watch my boundaries, though. I had learned.

10

It was a typical group of volunteers—mostly elderly, and painstaking in their meal preparation—and I immediately felt bad about my comment to Colter about the cuisine. The other female parolee residents represented the usual cross-section; clearly a long road in each case, fill in the details, but spirits high. We are the Hope House, after all, and everyone had jobs, even if they ranged between a car wash and a motel.

"We were up at the Legislature today," I announced to everyone, but especially to Colter.

"No, not you?" she replied, taking the bait.

"Yes indeed. Did you go up with us that time, way back? I can't remember."

"No," she answered. "But I heard about it. Crusita could not stop talking about it."

"Crusita did a great job. We didn't get any money out of it, but she silenced that committee room. You could have heard a pin drop. Remember that knot she had on her forehead?"

"We called her Volcano. It looked like a little volcano."

"You folks are so subtle. How mean."

"*She* was mean."

"Whatever. She did a great job that day, that's all I know. Usually, nobody pays attention, there's talking in the room, and it was the end of the day. But when in a quiet voice she started talking about her life, people shut up."

"She's had a hard road," Colter shrugged.

"What, *nine* kids?"

"Something like that."

"All in different orphanages across the West?"

"Something like that."

I remembered Colter's issues in that regard and swiftly changed course. "Anyway," I began, "she *had* that room. And the senators on the committee, they were sitting up in their chairs. And she was crying, swearing that she could make it this time, and thanking everyone for their forgiveness, et cetera."

"I thought you were a private charity," one of our volunteers asked. "Why ask the government for money?"

"Because it's there," I replied. "And we do the state's business, don't you think? Trying to whip this group into shape." I winked at the volunteer. "Get them out of their crazed, crime-spree ways." There was laughter around the table. "Actually," I continued, "this time it is different. We are having some real cash flow issues. Not because these fine women are not paying their rent, because they are."

"Seems to me that the government would save money if these gals were not in prison." our volunteer replied.

"Exactly."

"Maybe you should bring it up to the Legislature." Colter interjected. "He could represent."

"Oh, no," our volunteer answered. "I stay out of politics."

"That's fine," I assured him. "Cesare did a great job today. And our program should speak for itself."

"Chapman," Colter continued, "do you have a girlfriend yet?"

"Next question," I replied, reddening. "You know my situation."

"He has issues around commitment," she teasingly announced to the assembled.

"Now wait a second."

"See how he is blushing?" More laughter.

"Look, it's complicated," I began. "I would fill you in on my long, sad story if we had a few hours. But I have been dating again."

"What's her name?" Colter asked.

"Whose name? Oh, you mean Emily? Emily. It's been well over a year. Closer to two."

"That long?" Colter replied. "And you haven't asked her to marry you yet?"

"Wait a second."

"Boy, you *would* be a handful. I need to talk with her."

"I am not afraid of commitment. You know about my situation with Kit."

"Sure."

"Anyway," I said, moving the conversation along, "the young man did really well today. Cesare. Which is a good thing, because the stakes are high."

"How come we never get a chance to meet any of these male residents, like Cesare?" Colter asked mischievously.

"Oh, come on," I said quickly. "We are *not* going back to those times. Are you kidding me?"

"It was fun."

"Right. What Colter is referring to," I began to clarify for the rest of the table, "is that we used to have male and female residents of Hope House in the same facility."

"Oh, that doesn't sound too smart," one of the volunteers piped in.

"We had no choice. Zoning and such. Until we could expand, and at least separate...."

"It wasn't all that bad," Colter protested. "We have to figure out ultimately how to deal with men anyway, don't we, girls?" The other residents seemed a bit distracted, not sure what to say in this kind of conversation.

"Yeah, maybe, but not *immediately* after prison," I replied. *"Duh."*

"I gather there were problems?" another volunteer asked innocently.

"Problems?" At this point, I knew that I should redirect the conversation, which is probably easy to do when surrounded by elderly volunteers and jumpy ex-felons. "Well, here, too, if we had a couple of hours, I could fill you in."

But there was Colter, who wanted to pursue this subject. "We liked coming to Hope House," she began. "It was definitely the most popular program inside the walls. The girls used to talk about it on the cell pod."

"Okay, whatever. Let's just say that it is markedly better this way."

It was fantastic to have her back.

11

My newspaper interview was a barrel of laughs—back around endorsement time—though I put up a credible effort. I was told repeatedly that I had little chance, that my *Democratic* affiliation would obstruct any softening on *the* one and only paper. It started out amiably enough, joking with the three men, the feeling of being summoned, and it being terribly early in the morning. Then, the tight-lipped expressions set in on all three of them, and the questions ensued.

"Mr. Murphy," one of them began, "you have spoken often in your campaign literature about the need to improve our public schools. Specifically, how would you accomplish this?"

"Oh, yes," I replied. "That. Well, uh, it's just so large a task. It's hard to know where to begin."

"Give us an example," he continued, in not necessarily a friendly tone.

"Well … it's not just about spending more money." I began, waiting for the memorized points to call up on the screen of my mind. Like the phrases in that eight-ball toy. "We somehow have to get results—accountability—for the dollars spent."

"*And?*" *Was* I that bad?

"And, of course, we need to pay our teachers. We can't be losing them to surrounding states, like we are. This one woman I dated, for example. She left for Texas, where she could make twice as much. I feel this *personally.*" Polite smiles. "But I would ask you," I continued. "How can we secure accountability from parents, and *their* responsibility? How does one do that? It can't very well be legislated, can it?"

"Okay, then." They were only being polite at this point.

"I'm sorry," I added. "I'm just not a morning person." Did I actually say that?

"Well," one of them continued, "how about another area?"

"Sure. Go ahead."

"I see also from your campaign material that you work in the charitable sector. How does that kind of work prepare you for public service?" They must have felt sorry for me at this point. "How will that serve you if you should be elected to the State Legislature?"

"Well," I began, not needing the points on the screen that were not materializing anyway for this one. "Obviously, from doing the kind of work that I do, I know this community—and its problems—very well. Intimately. From the prisons to the homeless shelters, et cetera. And I am constantly talking about Hope House to local churches. Some big ones that are in the district, I might add."

"Oh, really," one of them said, smiling. "That could maybe help you in a couple of weeks?"

"I don't know," I shrugged. "Maybe so. It's like I have been very fortunate to have been able to make service my vocation in this community." Bingo, at last, the merciful screen. "My running for District 10 is a logical extension of my decades' worth of involvement in our state's hardest problems. And the importance of giving back, of course, I learned from my parents and all of that."

Silence in the windowless room.

"Okay, then. Anything else that you would like to add?"

"Just that ... I have upside. If given the opportunity. Your paper's endorsement would really help."

"Well, thanks for coming in. We will make our decision soon. And good luck."

12

Of course, the paper loved her anyway, my opponent. Everybody loved her. And I have to confess that I felt some affection for her as well. What is it with this *bond* that you can feel for your opponent? She beat me—I lost—and yet, when I saw her just now in the marble hallway, we had the nicest exchange. Instant recognition, like a family member or something, and a flickering sense of nostalgia as she passed by. What is that about?

"Murphy, do you have a second?" It was O'Rourke, the supreme veteran of the hallways. The best lobbyist up here, hands down.

"Of course."

"I was just in the Pro Tem's office, looking over the budget. You are not in there."

"Okay."

"If I were you," O'Rourke continued, looking at me through his aviator glasses, distracted but very present (I could not help but notice all of the inked phone numbers on the back of his hand, even past his wrist), "I would get to him ASAP. Tell him it's not much money in the scheme of things. It could be a line in the Corrections Budget; you could bury it somewhere."

"We have the bill that Senator Cohen is carrying. Asking for the same amount."

"That's fine, but that really doesn't do you any good."

"Oh."

"You want to be in Senate Bill 2. It's the state budget."

"But it's still early in the session, right?"

He paused. "Have you ever met the Pro Tem? Does he know you?"

"No."

Silence. "You want this funding, right?"

"We are going to have to close if we don't get it."

"I got the message."

Like much up here, avenues and paths are hidden. O'Rourke is a supreme navigator of these different routes and knows the inside game better than anyone. If he counsels that we are in trouble, we are in trouble. I kept thinking of what it would mean if Hope House ceased to exist: Colter, Cesare, and the many others that have come to us would have to take their stories elsewhere, take their chances alone in some weekly apartment with the craziness just outside. But more than that, we had worked hard to create this program—got the neighborhood and local businesses to accept our presence, even support it—and I just could not conceive of shutting our doors, asking our residents to leave, informing the churches that they no longer needed to bring dinner, et cetera. I suppose we would sell the compound, with its three small houses and surrounding barren lot. The board would have some ideas on that, I am sure. Just so tenuous, charity: making the payroll every week, going to the post office every day for the long-awaited foundation check, preying upon everyone I know as a potential donor. We cannot admit to failure, not in this case.

Unlike my political effort, which I can readily admit was a failure. You either win or lose, bottom line. However, we were cresting in late October, I know we were. The nice family up the road who did that fund-raiser for me—the Governor was there, with his bodyguards and black limo. Guest to this old-time, revered political tradition, and I did my best to honor that in my brief but maybe credible speech. I must have had *some* chance, otherwise the Barela family would not have gone to all that trouble—mariachi band, invitations, two hundred dollars a person. Maybe the Governor's people were behind it, as they were doing the same polling we were—there was an opportunity to pick up a seat if it all fell right. How strange: we would now like to introduce this dude from Iowa that nobody knows except that he is crazy enough to walk our neighborhoods in the hot sun. Some Irish name. And he is a Democrat, which is all that we need to know.

That was a good moment for me. There were the Governor, esteemed former legislators, longtime neighborhood politicos, the mariachi band, my lovely girlfriend Emily: all eyes on me. "Thank you, everyone," I said, as the Governor handed me the microphone, "I know it is getting late, and I will not keep you." And then it just came out, real nice, what I had nervously rehearsed all day, in different versions. The grassroots tradition at stake established by the esteemed former Senator Baca, who had represented this very district and was in attendance tonight. The honor of being a newcomer and on the verge of possibly restoring this soulful tradition. The complete invisibility of the incumbent, and my joke about being bitten *three* times in two weeks by the unchained dogs of the Valley. And, in conclusion, public policy definitely matters, the more we slog away how evident it becomes, and of course if elected you will know who your senator is. The name is Murphy. And I am a Democrat.

Sky-high when it was over, my campaign manager grinning as proof, and then everyone filing home. The bulging envelopes, and I could not help but hop up and down with some of the guests still in attendance, and of course my inner circle young and well-meaning and dazed like me with the prospect of our own adulthood. Off to the Hacienda Bar to celebrate, no more calls to be made, and only two weeks before Election Day.

At least I did not go blank that night, like I did during that last debate or forum or whatever it was called. At that moment, nothing but the sound of my own booming pulse as I surveyed the faces and the timekeeper's light. *The question again, please?* I apologized and then the screen lit up as I remembered what I had intended to say or had crammed all afternoon long in an attempt to be authoritative and believable. These were largely issues that I had never considered on any level, emblematic of how I was perhaps not a good fit for the district as the newspaper had bluntly stated in their endorsement of my opponent. Green zones and easements and the leasing of development rights, and always the three-tiered licensure system for educators that needed to be clarified. Thank God, there were only the usual twenty-five people in attendance—and no press. Plus, I did have some company in my faltering amid the assembled candidates. I probably did okay for a challenger as I tried to keep my attention away from my opponent's beautiful jet-black hair, and the polish of her conventional and very grownup world. Was this obvious to everyone? They could *not* have known about my recurring dream with her, where we are orphaned and waifish children together and I want to show her the secret clearing in the woods. Very innocent—just the bond of complete opposites and how sad the choices can become, the ones we make; how estranged we become from our own possibility.

I have tried to explain some of this to Emily—this unsettling bond you can feel with your enemy—but she was largely consumed with the more fundamental dilemma of why on earth a person would actually do this to themselves. Run for political office, that is.

13

The problem with me is that I am at least a decade older than people take me for, not that I am complaining. It's just that it is yet one more source of confusion in what I present to the world. And people my immediate age, both men and women, have seemed to drop off into oblivion, or they simply do not go out anymore. Therefore, I am usually way older than my immediate pals—men and women—which might not seem like a big deal, but it sneaks up on you. It is not as if I am some aging roué clinging desperately to his youth, honestly—I am 43, and if I have not married, there are reasons for that, legitimate ones. I frankly do not like to go out much—just dinner and some drinks afterwards—and I definitely do not like to stay out late. Just ask Adonis or Rashad, my basketball chums, who increasingly call me the *old white man,* as once again I decline their invitation to the late hour downtown club. "He's in lock-down anyway," Rashad would say in reference to Emily. "Plus, he is in bed by nine on a normal evening."

But Rashad and Adonis are on a whole different level— what, do I have *twenty* years on Rashad? And they look sharp in their pressed khakis and sports shirts, emerging from their polished sports cars, chrome gleaming. "That's another thing," Adonis would say, echoing our friend. "When are you going to get some different clothes? I mean, the suit and tie has got to go. And answer your cell phone sometime. That's why you have it, dumbass."

At this point I would weakly reply, "I'm working on that. I just don't like to be interrupted."

And then Adonis would grow even more furious. "Interrupted? From what? Your five-figure deals?"

Rashad the peacemaker would then intervene. "Leave the man alone. He's my hero." Then we would give each other our secret handshake. Then we would talk about our potentially triumphant city league team that I still wanted to call The Blind Pigs.

"I ain't no Blind Pig," Adonis replied testily.

"That may be," Rashad interjected, looking directly at Adonis, "but you shot like one this morning."

And so on, as we played pool, early in *their* evening, and me always looking for the right moment to exit.

It is truly not as if I *want* to be conspicuous—with the unsettling fact of my chronological age—but where are my peers? At home with their families, the rhythm of child-rearing, ports of entry that I have ignored; strange, my lack of interest in that. But it is not as if I ever thought it through to any great degree, nor have I been ruled by some elaborate ideology other than an instinctive refusal. Early on, a clear voice inside saying: "No way am I ever going to sign on to *this.*" And *this* being expansive—covering just about everything—that it gathers momentum and simply becomes my current station in life. Bachelor. Local curiosity, especially if you choose to put your life out there for public interpretation.

But I always thought I was rather invisible in my defiance, so it came as a shock when others noticed my behavior. Like Adonis, or my campaign manager, incensed at my unwillingness to answer the phone. I probably fare best with relative strangers—maybe that's why I can do this political thing. Introduce myself in flattering afternoon light, wanting simply a vote, not a *relationship*. And then on to the next door. I think it might have whacked me out a bit, all of those repeated and brief conversations. And I have got to visit the *patrones* at their jolly breakfast gathering before their worst suspicions are confirmed, that I am not serious about this political stuff, that it was only a whim on my part. Manuel will be angry with me, as he had a Murphy bumper-sticker on all of his vehicles, including his work truck.

But so what if I have a different life? Almost by default, it would seem. By now, my nephews and nieces have multiplied several times over; and if not for Emily, God help me, I might be a pathetic lonely man. My parents had long since given up on me before they passed, or at least resigned themselves to whatever it is that I presented to them, their rebellious son. Apparently, I was named after the colorful bachelor uncle on my mom's side. So, it is not unprecedented in Murphy-land.

One fine thing about non-profit work is the people who are attracted to work in this area, and Hope House has been no exception to that. Niall, for example— a thirty-something extremely educated fellow straight from Ireland. He was quick to anger and politically extreme, with his buzz cut and Gaelic tattoos. I never pressed him on what he actually did after college in his home country—like me, he probably had years that he did not feel like discussing—but I assumed that he was involved with some anarchist-like group, given comments he would make about *the rich* and how they would get theirs *someday*. Especially after a couple of beers. But he was good with our volunteers, my board loved him—we all liked to hear him talk, with that thick Irish accent. How he ended up at our doorstep I have no idea. But advocating for criminals was a natural for Niall.

Things had settled down on the Hope House front after my return from the freight trains, at least on the staffing level. Macey, our new Executive Director, was a steadying influence at the very least. She would bring her dog, Charlie, to the office, and he soon became extremely popular with our residents. She told me repeatedly that she was not much of an extrovert, that she loved to write grants and stay on top of our paperwork, and in that way, we were an ideal team. She had absolutely no interest in going to the Legislature, or in schmoozing with donor prospects. But she was great with our volunteer cooks each evening, and likewise very good with the board.

One downside of non-profit staffing is its ephemeral nature. People like Niall are essentially passing through, on to the next idealistic phase in their lives. (Niall vanished as mysteriously as he appeared.) And when we had someone like Macey in place, we wanted desperately to ink her to a long-term contract, as you would with a talented professional athlete. But she had yet to start a family, and her husband was so-so about the relentless demands presented by our unusual household of ex-convicts. Maybe he would come around in time.

14

It's time to talk about Emily.

When I first saw her at the local coffee shop, I could not take my eyes off her, there at the table across the way, reading a novel, sipping tea. She was not oblivious to my attention, and would periodically look up and smile, looking directly at me. Nervously, I thought of what pretext I could conjure to go over and introduce myself—these random encounters were always unpredictable, and rejection tended to linger in my psyche. But her light brown hair was so beckoning, and her incandescent green eyes, and her lovely petite form. Plus, there was the open invitation in *her* flirtation as well.

I risked a visit to her table, pretending interest in the novel that she was reading, and we were off into the dance of infatuation. She was so my type: artistic, non-linear, small, rebellious—searching for her own life as well. I was just very physically attracted to her, from the get-go. And I must have registered in her predisposition that way as well, as she did comment on my curly hair.

Our courtship began, both of us stepping over or largely ignoring the warning signs. For me: her zany past that included many lovers she seemed to relish telling me about in graphic detail. For her: the handful that I apparently was (according to Colter), what with my attentions elsewhere (translated, *work* … *but* not entirely confined to that area, of course). She had never been married, had no children, and was younger than I, but not by that much. We mirrored each other in the important ways: our jealousy, our specific wounds from the past, our longing for an elevated connection. But I was not enthused about her reliance upon psychotropics. And then she, of course, was insistent upon how I should go on them as well, given how "nervous" I was about everything.

But I forgave her for that. I wanted to be with her, to have her, physically, *in that way*. We would have these long, drawn-out fights—starting at the restaurant, where she would accuse me of flirting with the waitress. And then it would escalate into tromping around *her* impulsive past, her choices in men. As she knew that would get me going. And then one of us would storm out of the restaurant, flip a coin. And then two hours later, I would hear the sound of her battered Volvo outside my apartment, in the cul-de -ac. And then we would pardon each other, tears, and upstairs we would go to my bedroom, where we would really get down to the business of forgiving each other, proving it repeatedly.

Anyway, I was crazy about that girl from the start.

Our holiday special event was our moment in the community when we could display our success stories and make bank in the process. I would never coach our resident speakers, though maybe I should have, in retrospect. For every Reggie, there was that resident who shamelessly pitched our audience to help pay for her daughter's entrance into private school. "She has been accepted into the academy," Patti said, "but with me just getting out of prison and all, I can't afford it." Our well-heeled dinner goers shifted uncomfortably in their seats, though a good many of them were criminal defense attorneys and judges who knew the drill. Happily, nobody responded to her request after the dinner with an anonymous check. And then there was one of our first speakers, Jerry, after we had been open for less than a year: "There I was," he began, "in solitary confinement for murdering a guy who would not pay for his drugs." Jerry was a muscular guy with the expected tattoos on his forearms and slicked-back hair like Elvis, who was one of his musical heroes. I cringed as he continued: "They said I would never get out of prison. They said I would never amount to anything. But here I am." At that moment he looked at me and my table, and I telepathically, with some accompanying gestures, urged him to say something about remorse. But he didn't. Polite applause and mercifully on to the next part of the dinner program.

15

I should mention here how weird it was to have all of those dear campaign volunteers—a majority of them new acquaintances—on the phones seven deep at the donated accountant's office, talking about Murphy's "Way to the Brighter Tomorrow," or whatever it was that we were telling people. My campaign manager was always tightlipped and serious when he distributed the identical scripts to our callers. Of course, I wanted to be anywhere else but there, having to walk down the hallway and endure my own name in stereo, wincing at the public nature of it all. "He has the experience and the vision, Murphy does—can we count on your support?" It seemed way over-the-top pushy, especially the last bit about asking for someone's undying allegiance on the basis of a random, three-minute conversation; why not just go ahead and ask for their credit card number, or ATM access code? And then there was, "We happen to have the candidate *himself here* with us tonight if you should have any questions for him." Right. "Chapman is against animal abuse in any form. And he strongly believes in the dignity of all species." And so forth.

Where I wanted to be instead was out on the streets, walking solitary in the early summer evening, introducing myself relentlessly door to door, and going for a personal record of household contact; *not* to be there listening to the evidence of my own duplicity, to have these well-meaning volunteers roped into my own private ambition, the prospect of losing a real possibility. But then they were *my* posse. The diminutive, retired union guy with his smoker's voice, for example, checking me out early on. "I want to know three things," he had said. "Where is your wife? Where are your signs? And where are your mailings?" He ultimately became a diehard on my behalf, as I patiently answered each question to his satisfaction. As the weeks passed, his loyalty and commitment almost made me uneasy—he would always show up, always finish his phone list, and along with Manuel had my signs plastered throughout the district. I suppose it was probably just enough that I was a Democrat. I wanted desperately to thank him, and the legion of others, and the best way to do that was by winning my race.

But it was not easy, the public nature of it all, even on this level of local politics. The billboards were tough—how many days did it take me to actually look at one? I would drive past quickly, eyes averted. The old-timers in the neighborhood, like Manuel and the Barela family, they must have been truly puzzled by my appearance: Who *is* this guy? And where did he come from? Manuel confided as much, two months into my candidacy, with that salesman's grin of his. "I have never seen you around here before," beckoning me politely out of the Spring neighborhood parade. "Who are you?" I did my best to answer his question. He kind of smiled and shook his head.

When I finally pulled it together and visited Manuel and the *patrons—los viejos cabrones*—it went something like this:

"Hey!" someone said, the conversation having immediately stopped upon my entrance. "Look who's here. Is there an election coming up?" It was Mario.

"Hey," I began sheepishly. "How are you all?"

"What brings you in here?" Mario was not necessarily kidding. Coffee cups all around, the sugar-laden breakfast rolls.

"Well," I hesitated, "I *live* here. I get hungry, too, like you guys."

"Leave him alone, Mario." Gaspar was always my champion, softer than the rest. "He almost pulled it off."

"That's what I'm saying," Mario countered. "He would have if he'd only listened to us. *Escucha*" he scolded, pointing to his ear.

"That's not true," I protested. "I listened to you guys—are you kidding me?"

"She was ripping down your signs." It was Gaspar again. "My sister caught them. In broad daylight. I think it was her campaign manager—that kooky guy, what's his name?"

"Or her husband," someone added. There was laughter.

"Well, she must have been nervous," I replied.

"She's never been to my door," another added. His name was Loyola.

"Well," Mario continued, "are you going to sit down?"

"Yes, I was."

"Get this man some coffee."

"Thanks," I said, faking enthusiasm for the expected weak concoction.
"No *problema*," Mario replied. He was the putative leader of the bunch, and it was a big deal for me when he clamped

two of my signs on his storefront fence. "You ran a good race, *huero*," he continued. "She's hard to beat."

"Too bad you had what's-his-name at the top of the ticket," someone added.

"I out-performed him in most of the district," I could not help but quickly reply. "Definitely here in the Valley."

"He was too soft," Mario said, reaching for the coffeepot. "Goddamned Republicans."

"My sister saw this guy pull up," Gaspar began, back to the yard sign issue. "A real nice car. Big fancy thing. And then this well-dressed man gets out. Suit and tie and everything. Then he yanks your sign right out of her front yard and puts it in his car. Then he looks right at her and drives off. She would have said something, but she thought it must have been one of your people."

"Why would my people do that?" I replied.

"Somebody owes you five dollars," Mario laughed. "Is that what one of those signs cost these days?"

"Something like that," I answered. "They're not cheap."

"Who *was* that?" Gaspar asked, referring back to his sister's encounter.

"I'm not sure," I replied, truly wanting to change the subject. "But I think that there are only two possible suspects."

"*Su esposa*?" Gaspar said, shaking his head.

"A man like that, making all of that money," Mario added. "She has surrounded herself with a strange crowd," I said in my opponent's defense. "Starting with him, I suppose. Very fundamentalist. She, on the other hand, is nice and reasonable when you talk with her in person."

"She has just lost her way," Loyola interjected. "It happens."

"She used to be a Democrat."

"That's what I mean," Loyola replied. Then, to the others, "Remember when Francisco crossed over?" There was much nodding around the table. "There's lots of opportunity on *that* side. Especially if you're brown."

"And have dark eyes," someone said. More laughter.

"Francisco got trounced," Gaspar interjected, "by a lot more than this young fellow did."

"I'm not young," I clarified. There was more laughter. "Or not *that* young," I added.

"Okay, we believe you," Mario teased. "Obviously we are old. Right, everyone?"

"*Los cabrones viejos*," someone added.

"And it colors our experience," Mario continued. "If you're not young, then we are *really* old."

"I think Francisco probably regretted the whole experience," Loyola continued.

"He stopped coming here," someone added.

"We wouldn't let him through that door," Mario said, pointing to the restaurant's portal.
"Didn't he change back?" Gaspar asked. "Run as a Democrat next time?"

"He had *issues*," Mario said with finality. "Isn't that how you say it these days? *Issues?*"

"You have to at least know which side you're *on*," Gaspar replied. "I can respect someone who doesn't agree with me. But don't be all over the map."

"All over the stratosphere," Loyola echoed. There was more laughter at the table.

"How's the *coffee?*" Mario asked me.

"Fine," I said, lying. "You guys don't drink any of the fancy stuff?"

"Oh, what?" Mario answered. "The mocha frappachinos?"

"Yes. A new place just opened down the street."

"We are kind of settled in our *ways,*" Gaspar replied. "Aren't we, men?" There was nodding.

"Are you going to run again?" Loyola asked.

"I don't know," I replied. "The district has changed, from what I understand. I'm not into just running all of the time. Whenever there's an election, like some people do."

"Like Francisco," Mario interjected.

"Yeah. But I promise I won't change parties. As tempting as it might be."
"They really did screw up the district," Mario mused. "We were stupid to agree with those bastards. Damned gerrymandering."

"It's all about the lines," Gaspar said with finality, "where they are drawn."

Ultimately the breakfast ended, and I promised that I would not be a stranger, that I would come by even if there was no election. I followed Manuel to his double-wide a few blocks away, with its neatly manicured lawn and abundance of flowers. He wanted me to pick up my remaining signs.

Being away from my fund-raising duties during my political campaign was not exactly helpful to Hope House's monthly bottom line. The board had been generous to grant me a leave of absence, acknowledging my private ambition. Donations to Hope House were never far from my mind, but inevitably there was the immediate concern of winning my race. Plus, my campaign manager was always pressing me on meeting my fund-raising goals, aware of the accumulating bill with his political consulting firm. I knew that I was lucky to have them—that they didn't take on just any candidate—but I have never been good with taking expenses seriously, both personal and professional. I kept assuring him that I was, in fact, a *professional* fund-raiser, and not to worry so much, that the money would be there. Inside, however, I felt uneasiness about asking my Hope House donors to contribute to my political campaign. I knew that the whole asking for money routine was, by its very nature, *relational*— whether it involved a charitable donation slip, or a campaign contribution. My campaign manager would tell me repeatedly: we need the money to get your message out, *money is message*. It just seemed selfish to switch gears like that, to make it about *me* instead of Hope House.

But I did.

16

Of course, I was, and am, attracted to her—to my opponent, that is—but it is not as if I would ever let such a sentiment be known. I see her in the Rotunda, and it is a charged pleasantry, on my end, at least; all of the other tension recedes (stolen signs, negative mailings, the drudgery of her being an *enemy* for five months). She smiles and I drink in her memory, minus the bad sensation of losing that night. I knew that we were in trouble early that evening, despite the optimism of early national polls. I have this crazy notion of what it would be like just to hang out with her, without the complexity of our respective hostile worlds. An even crazier notion of going shopping with her—this misunderstood talent of mine—and we could definitely make some headway with her "look." We would start off by ridding her of the pantsuits and obvious penchant for red; we would hit the boutiques on her behalf, and the hip used-clothing stores as well; and she would surprise herself with denim and nicely cut natural fabric.

I am weird. Duly noted.

But everyone would benefit from it—even her husband and kids—as the intention on both ends would be pure, in the spirit of fun. An escape from the partisanship box. And I could tell Emily about it, though maybe that would be pushing it on the jealousy front. My opponent would feel better about herself. Maybe an acknowledgment on her end of the life she had *before* she made that turn into whatever she is living now.

I am an odd fellow, I have to admit, in this, my only life. My own weaknesses I have come to know, and yet there is restorative power in relapse. The larger picture, however, is a different matter. How can it be named? So vast and relentless and predictable, the red and the blue reducing everything into the logic of affiliation? I have plenty of friends on the other side—family even—yet it does not help me to understand them. I grow weary of the partisan ranting, but what is to be done about it? It is just that their faces get tight—*their side*—their memories perhaps colored by what did not happen for them? Or simply following along with what they were taught by their parents? Growing in numbers they are, as how easy it is to reject your own possibility. Plus, that damned channel blaring night and day with its venom. Up against this equation what can be done? How does one coax or conjure a brighter world of possibility without being ridiculed? Let alone, how can one convince the other half to at least soften their opinions? I am sure it goes both ways, though. A hard and unyielding map, red versus blue—menacing—turning away from each other like a doomed, warring couple.

"My therapist says that I should break up with you." It was Emily.

"Great," I answered, wearily. "Is that the same guy that pushes those meds your way?"

"He is very good. You should consider seeing him as well."

"Please. We've been through this." I could feel the beginning of a familiar escalation.

"I just wish you'd look at some things. Your behavior in certain areas."

"It's not like I don't acknowledge that I have issues." Here I could not help but think of Mario, and his use of the same word.

"You are just so distant. So *consumed*."

"Try running for political office."

"That's a choice you make."

"It just has its side effects. You know I'm mad for you."

"Then why were you looking at the waitress the other night? Right in front of me?"

"It wasn't on that level, I swear. I know her brother."

"And where do you go when you don't call me back?"

"I am just busy with the campaign ... as I've told you many times. Were you able to paint today?" Here just trying to shift the conversation. Not evading, let the minutes reflect.
She paused. She was wearing that green top that I bought for her two weeks previously. And the faded jeans that fit her so well. It was starting on my end.

"It's just that I don't know if I can trust you. You have so many others in your life. These *women*."

"Are you familiar with the concept of *friendship?*" I protested. "Just because your past is dark in that respect."
It was late afternoon, approaching the time when I should be out walking the district. We were in our favored local

coffee shop, as Emily had figure drawing to go to as well. We stopped talking.

"I'm sorry." I said, reaching out for her delicate hand. "I didn't mean it like that."

"It's your issue," she shot back, not moving an inch. "I presume that you are an adult man. Though you really don't act like it."

"I am just trying to process who you are."

"Don't do me any favors," Emily shot back.

Thirty minutes later we were in my apartment, upstairs. We had both successfully managed to hurt each other, in a by now familiar way, and it was time to make amends. But not in our usual fashion. We both agreed it was better this time to simply hold each other, which we did, and as it turned out it was quite lovely, just listening to some version of Gaelic-feeling music and simply being present to each other. I loved how her small body felt next to mine. Inevitably, we both started crying, and it was just very special to silently witness each other in this way, instead of the usual acting out of our respective anger or jealousy or whatever it was that made us want each other so badly. Figure drawing would have to wait. And then too, my walking the district.

17

The division was out there, sure enough, and it was hard not to experience it firsthand as I walked through my beloved maps. Most people were polite, regardless of partisan affiliation, but you could feel how tightly drawn the sides were. Of course, Independent voters were the prize—or Decline to States—but that stated registration was not necessarily an accurate one; people don't like to be pigeon-holed. The other side had its zealots, and I got to where I could almost predict the imminent tirade. "Son," that one guy said, emerging from his house and closing the door. "How *could* you be a Democrat? Have you seen what they do to the skulls of babies?" Whiskey or something on his breath, he moved closer to me. "Democrats are degenerates, plain and simple." I moved back from him and replied, "Wait a second, pal. What kind of comment is that?" He stood there, guarding his house. "Get out of here!" he exclaimed. "No vote for you here." I could not help but respond, trying to calm myself. "This is a civic process, buster. I don't want your fucking vote anyway." I was angry, trembling. "That's good," he replied. "Because you're not getting it. Now get off my property and *don't* come back here again." I turned and walked away.

They tended to be men, these types, going on about *fetuses* and *baby-killing* and of course the ubiquitous, *"What about the father?"* Oh, please, I would mutter to myself, enough already. I guess that's why I'm a Democrat. Our walk lists were kind of primitive, I suppose: R, D, or I, and how often a person actually voted. Their age and gender. I tried not to profile, but it was impossible not to after several months of this. Yards and gate systems were often the tip-off: the inaccessible steel fence usually meant Republican, along with American flag decals on the front door and a kick-ass alarm system. Democrats were more defined by what was absent: no slowly rotating surveillance camera, for example, or No Soliciting sign. But my side had its hate as well. "Can you believe what an idiot he is?" did grow tiresome, as if I would *of course* participate in this kind of ridicule, being the Democratic candidate. My dad went to school with this idiot's father, for Chrissakes; he was there when he was born.

That should have been an asset in our campaign strategy, as geared towards the swing voter we were with our entire effort: nowhere on my teeth-whitened flier would you find any mention of party. I am only an amiable and maybe colorful guy running as myself—tailored specifically for the Independents, the Decline to States, who were everywhere, presumably, though enigmatic in their ways. How well they listened and even thanked me for the effort, this presentation before new houses with the dogs safely in the back, this quiet Republican planet. I walked it, though, cheery with my handshake and sincerity.

My poor campaign manager, unsure of *what* to make of me, let alone how to present me to voters. I did not mean to be flippant with his initial questionnaire, but how else is one supposed to answer a question like, "What makes you laugh?" (A question like this does, dork.) And yes, clothes-shopping for my girlfriend Emily *is* my hobby, as well as picking out vintage clothes for myself. Concerned, he gave me a duplicate questionnaire answered by one of their legions of winning candidates. "Dude," I said to him in the office that day, "I will *never* be the person of *these* answers. For instance, yes, I did get into trouble as a boy, but it had

nothing to do with my *boundless curiosity* or my *love of animals.*
Are you kidding me? I understand that he had to save the
mustangs, even as a boy, and that his innocent desire to cut
class to follow their movements was noble indeed, and it
would make him an excellent elected official. I, on the other
hand, was locked into the cruiser's back seat because at age
fourteen I was wild and thirsty and publicly intoxicated—"

He interrupted me here, putting the file down. "Are you
serious about this, or not?" I nodded.

"Do you realize how many people are watching this race?
Your race? And watching our performance for you as well?"

I was feeling bad at this point, not wanting to hurt or
embarrass anyone. "Okay, then," I answered, "I *am* serious.
And I will prove it to you. I will walk like a fiend."

"It isn't just walking." He sighed. "You have to raise money,
keep up with our expense. And don't forget the phone
banking."

I did improve, however, and by October I was right there in
the tracking poll, the race a dead heat, as the Governor had
mentioned that night at the Barela fund-raiser. My campaign
manager grew slightly less nervous with each passing debate
or candidate forum or important interview (except for the
newspaper endorsement one), as he was always unsure of
what he would get from me. I would tell him, in one of our
countless briefings, that I am not much good in the morning.
"Dude," he replied one day, "it's after one o'clock." Election
night was hard, and the hopes were high from those inflated
polls back East. But I was unsettled by what I saw with my
own eyes, waving as a candidate at the troublesome polling
place (in *not* a friendly precinct) as the voting line would not
go down. A two-hour wait at this site, in vivid contrast to
my sleepy Democratic strongholds. This was not good, and
I called him again, seeking reassurance. *These are not my people,*

I told him. And still they kept coming—that RV brandishing American flags, with the national anthem turned up loud— quietly doing their killing of dreams like mine, making their presence felt. I waved all morning long, as this was where the voters were. I needed to call him again, to voice my concern. "Dude," he answered calmly. "Don't worry. These early results are awesome. Bode well."

Back on the Hope House front, since my return from hobo- land, we continued to be fortunate. As if we had some kind of benevolent force making sure that we did not lose our effort. Take the case of Leroy Flowers, for example, a legendary local athlete who actually played professional football. Halfback, for nearly a decade. In our state university Athletic Hall of Fame, as well as celebrated by his one and only professional team (in their Ring of Honor as well). I remember watching him on Sunday television as a boy. Quiet, modest, soft-spoken, and *very* interesting—he had an artistic streak that manifested in his writing poetry and performing in local plays. Somehow, he came to our perpetually tenuous effort and was soon to become my board president. "Murphy," he would softly tease, "what kind of trouble are we in now? Do we have any money left? Is Raphael on the loose again?"

So, we had this *revered* African-American former gladiator on our side—there to speak for us—when Raphael or whomever ended up on the evening news. Obviously, I wanted him up at the Legislature, to help with our funding request, but he drew the line there. I had noticed early on how reluctant he was to be *Leroy Flowers*. After the autograph seeker had gone away, his polite role gave way to his truer, more introspective self. "I am sorry, Murphy, but that is just not my deal. Makes me want to take a shower after a day up there." Still, I was able to quickly state—in any presentation, before the microphone—without emphasis, as if it were no big thing, that "*Leroy Flowers is our board president.*" How could I resist asking him to record a robo-call on my behalf towards the end of my campaign? He has a deep, baritone voice—among his many other talents—and of course my campaign folks loved the idea. They gave him a simple script, and he dutifully went to the studio to record it: "*Hello, this is Leroy Flowers. I have come to know Chapman Murphy, and I believe that he would make a fine Senator. We need a voice like his up in Santa Fe.*"

In a campaign you never really know what messaging makes an impact, but this certainly didn't hurt.

18

I think I knew I was in love with Emily when we took our first trip together—back to the world of her origin. Semi-rural Virginia, but close enough to a big university and all of the intelligence that brings. We had gone into great detail about each other's upbringing, its tribulations and high points. Hers had unfolded with undisputed trauma, which was why she worked in the helping professions to support her painting. Her father had a difficult relationship with money, thinking he always had more than he actually had, and her beloved family farm met with inevitable foreclosure. Her siblings and her mother did their best to hold things together in the face of his gradual emotional unraveling—at least her education at the local Catholic girls' school was not impeded—but bad things were happening in that family. There was a year that she could not remember very well, when the county humane authorities came to possess the starving livestock. I am not clear on whether or not her father was ultimately charged with animal abuse, but there was a downward spiral for him in play that existed outside of the criminal justice system. The family was embarrassed, and he had a temper.

I remember walking the ridge with Emily above her former family property—what she always called *the farm*—the outbuildings and barn still in existence but freshly painted by the new family. We said nothing. She was crying.

"Oh, Chappie," she said, reaching for my arm, "I am *so* sad."

"It's okay, kiddo," I said, gripping her hand. "You did the best you could. Even *he* did, in his way."

"I don't know about that. He was mean. And crazy. I don't think he ever accepted that we had lost the farm. To him it was a just a streak of bad luck."

"Where did you go after that? I mean, as a family?"

"Well, we went with my mom, to her sister's. While dad was presumably getting the farm back. He needed to be alone. Which was just fine with us."

"Did he drink?"

"No. His problems were elsewhere. Like with this inflated sense that he was some kind of country gentleman. ... Do you realize what it was like to see our animals ... *like that?* As a child, my favorite horse?" Tears were running down her face.

"I am *so* sorry," I said, kissing her cheek, instinctively licking her tears, trying to make things better.

"I loved every one of those animals: we had a cow named Dusty. My horse named Smokey. Lambs ..."

"It's okay." I held her tighter.

"We *tried* to get his attention. We told him the animals were clearly starving, especially Smokey—his ribs were almost poking through. ... It was terrible. I don't know what *he* was seeing. ... Delusional he was. I know that now. His DSM could have been a number of things."

"It's okay, Emily. I love you so terribly much." Our eyes met. Hers were soft. "It kind of freaks me out, " I continued. "I don't know what to do with these feelings."

"Do you really?" she asked, looking directly into my eyes in a way that was both euphoric and terrifying. To me at least. "*Love* me and all of that?"

"You know I do."

"What about the others?"

"There are no others."

"Yes, there are. You scare me that way."

"What I feel right now," I began, with some vehemence, "I have never felt before. With anyone. And there certainly is not another woman in my life now."

"What about the past?"

"What about *your past*?" I winced, as I did not really mean for it to surface like that. I knew that this was something I had to work out for myself—we had established that, as a couple.

"Disregard that comment," I continued. "Isn't it enough that we've found each other?"

Emily said nothing, as we continued to embrace each other and kiss passionately. Finally, she broke it off. "Let's get out of here," she said, taking my hand and leading me back to the car.

"No argument here," I replied.

The trip was storybook: museums in the city, the adventure of fellow passengers beholding our romance on trains and planes, long candlelit evenings where our forgiving continued, with each time that we could not resist each other. Erotic shadows on the wall, the doomed effort to keep the volume down in deference to our unseen neighbors. Radiant breakfasts, with her hair just right, and her undeniably sexy form wherever we went—I would notice other men checking her out, and I did not exactly know how to respond to that. Her presence, just being next to her, was invariably thrilling to me, and I could not keep from touching her. And my affection was clearly welcomed by her and returned. I felt some kind of healing going on for me that I did not realize I needed, though clearly, I should have.

Anyway, that trip was early in the campaign, before the demands and events really kicked in. When the focus could be where it deserved to be. On us.

19

The Governor and his people were convinced that the only way to beat my opponent was to go negative—not that he had taken such great interest in my race, it was just on their radar screen. Especially after our poll that found it to be close, a dead heat even, within the statistical margin of error. The poll was expensive (I will get to some of that later), and I wondered who would actually take the time to answer such questions. But it did transform my campaign, this poll. Off I went to cash in on my new sudden visibility: trial lawyers, unions, the usual constituencies on my side. But the Governor and his emissaries did not mess around in these matters. A packet soon arrived at my apartment, with "CONFIDENTIAL" stamped on the top of its one-page cover summary. The focus was my opponent, and I found it to be unsettling, as I tossed it unread into the corner of my living room. This was definitely not my element, cynical wrongdoings described in a language belonging to other people. But to the Governor, and others, this was serious business. My campaign manager was upset when I finally answered the phone.

"Look," he said, after he had calmed a bit. "They have been on the phone with us all morning. We need to make a decision."

"Okay," I replied, keeping my concentration on an upcoming exit sign. "What's the issue?"

"Did you receive that package of opposition research?"

"Oh yeah, *that*. Seems kind of creepy to me."

"They want to use it."

"Use what?"

"The fact is, she lied. On the newspaper questionnaire."

"Yeah, but that can happen to anyone. You can get those kinds of things and not even know they exist, right?"

"The point they are making is that we need something to put us over the top. Technically you are behind."

"But I feel good about what we're doing. All we need is sixty percent of the Independents, right?"

"They're pros. They've been at it a long time. He's the Governor."

"What do they want us to do?"

"They want an attack piece. An extremely negative one."

"But why? Won't it backfire? What, are we supposed to believe that she is some kind of *criminal?* What is a summary judgment anyway? I don't even know what this stuff is."

"You are the candidate," my campaign manager sighed. "We can't make this decision for you."

"What decision?" I asked.

"The one authorizing this piece. They'll pay for it."

"That's good. Because I am way behind on paying you folks, as you know. That poll was a freakin' fortune."

"It's your decision."

"Can I call you back in five minutes?"

"No. You need to make it right now."

"I do? Shit." I had missed my exit. "I don't know. How am I supposed to know this stuff?"

"We have less than twelve days before the election. Plus, with early and absentee —"

"It might be too late anyway, right?" I said.

"No," he answered after a long pause. "In a race like this—they think we need a bounce."

"Okay. But I think it will backfire. Seriously, she's a nice person. Everybody knows that. She's just misguided, politically."

"So, what's your decision?"

"No!" I said with emphasis. By now I was on the shoulder of the highway, with traffic moving busily past. "I don't feel good about it. If I can't beat her without this brand of low maneuvering, then fuck it."

"Good," my campaign manager said. "We feel the same way. Now leave your goddamned phone on."

"Okay, okay," I replied.

As it turned out, the Governor's people were furious with our refusal and were quick to point out that, without his support, my numbers would not be where they were. Plus, there was the pointed reference to his sudden financial backing. All of this in the heated phone calls that followed our lofty choice. By their five o'clock deadline, we had conceded—the mailing was already going to press—and I felt compromised, like I had lost a part of my soul. My campaign manager agreed that it was an unfortunate aspect of this political business, but we really owed it to all of our backers to do everything we could to win the election. I just personally did not want to be around when it hit—we guessed it would take about three days before it would arrive in the mailboxes of District 10.

In the following days, I became morose and a bit robotic as I went about the campaigning: phone calls, door to door, an appearance or two. Of course, all of this was top secret. I could not confide in anyone even if I wanted to—except Emily, of course, but it's not like that was a fair position to put her in, baffled as she was by the whole endeavor. She just kept saying not to worry, that people will understand, that it is just politics. I did not sleep very well for a couple of nights, and I had no interest in previewing the actual piece in question. Overhearing my campaign manager on its content had been enough—something about a splintered photo of her, with the word LIAR plastered on the front side. I even thought about calling her—I had her cell number buried somewhere—but I did not because there were too many other things to occupy my time.

When it did ultimately hit, I survived okay, buried as it was among all of the other campaign literature from *everyone* in the election waning days. When it came to my mailbox, I recoiled at it before tossing the piece in the trash, feeling ashamed and disgusted with myself. As it turned out, there was a minimal response, either way—I received no angry phone calls or even accusing looks from my neighbors.

These local contests unfolded in this way, through the mailboxes, and of course the automated phone calls. When her equivalent mail piece arrived the following day—the one with the grainy photos ridiculing my very existence and implying that I was an ex-felon myself—I realized that I should take this as a compliment, as proof that I was running a strong race. Her portrayal of me was odd, I thought, and it did not offend me in the slightest. But I became concerned when I saw the look on my campaign manager's face.

"It's good," he said, turning her attack piece over. "Nice graphics. Much better than her other mail."

"Yes," I protested, "but how stupid it is. I never said those things. Not in *that way,* I mean."

"But it's effective nevertheless," he said in a monotone. "The bit about your lack of experience—"

"But I'm the challenger. *Of course,* I don't have experience."

"And the implied link to criminals," my campaign manager continued.

"It's my *job.* To help them, that is."

"No matter. It effectively contrasts you two."

"Well, to hell with it then. I was expecting much worse. This is it, right? It's too late for another piece?"

"I think so, but maybe not. There are ways. But in this election, everyone's voted by now. I've never seen anything like it."

20

I don't know why I needed to see Carlos badly—I should have been following O'Rourke instead, coaxing bits of prized information from his distracted being. We were *not* in the budget—Senate Bill 2—and that was worrisome. I kept being reassured by others that there were many ways to get into the budget, even in a short session, and that I should not be all stressed out. Certainly, I conveyed this same message to my board's Executive Committee, who welcomed such news; but I could tell that they were not entirely convinced. The bottom line was the bottom line, and we were in trouble. We needed the money.

"Hey, nice hat," I said, finding the chair next to Carlos at the bar.

"You like it?" he replied, taking it off. "I should let *you* try it on, but I don't think so."

"It's okay," I replied. "I'm not into hats."

"But this is a fine one—the felt imported, *ese*. From Andalusia. Like the running of the bulls. Pamplona."

"What are you doing in here?" I asked. "I mean, don't you have bills to track?"

"I'm doing it right here," he said, pointing to his sheet. "I do my best tracking in here, eh? With my other *trackers.*" There was laughter in the immediate vicinity, lobbyists doing the same thing. But despite the venue, and Carlos's aw-shucks attitude, it felt very serious in the bar. Like a library.

"I am going to buy you and your friends a round," I announced.

"No complaints here, friend." The others nodded, reviewing their respective lists. "Don't you have a holiday coming up? Your Cinco de Mayo?"

"It's not for a while yet. You have Irish in you, right?"

Everyone laughed. "Eee, yes. Black Irish. Carlos O'Griego." The drinks arrived. "You are not partaking?" Carlos asked me.

"It's only two o'clock."

"Your choice."

"I can't work the way you guys can—and drink at the same time, I mean."

"This is not work," he replied.

"Nonsense. You know exactly what's going on with that sheet there. How are you looking?"

"Not good," he shrugged, "but then, my clients will need me even more *next* year."

"I'm sure you're doing just fine."

"The Governor, he's got his own agenda."

"But you're good with him, right?" I asked.

"Maybe," Carlos shrugged. "What about you? How are things with your *vatos?*"

"Our program is in trouble. We need the money. You know the Pro Tem well, right?"

"Have you met with him?"

"Yes. But … I'm just another *advocate.*"

"He should be supportive. People in prison should get a break now and then. And you did run for office. As a Democrat."

"Yes, but it's a money thing. We need to be in that budget. Seriously. Can you talk to him? I know you have other priorities."

"For you, my Irish brother, of course I will. Just stay on him. Cannot be timid up here."

"You *are* good with the Governor, right?" I asked him, honestly just curious at this point.

"Who knows?" he shrugged again. "It's hard to read him."

"But you have access."

"Those days are over," Carlos answered. "It's a new era. Open government and shit. *Transparency.* "

"I don't think it's completely over, those days," I said. "I mean, look at this scene," I added, pointing to the surrounding room. "Those are real cigars over there. And the smoke is killing me."

"You are just like that Bat Masterson guy with your outfits," Carlos replied, "Where do you get those clothes, by the way? The Goodwill? Those ties went out years ago."

"They're called vintage stores. And thrift shops too."

"You might not want to be so flamboyant. If you run again, I mean."

"What do you mean by that?"

"You can make people nervous. You're by yourself all the time, wearing those outfits."

"These are just narrow ties. I don't wear *outfits*."

"You don't have a wife. No kids. You're not *from* here."

"Really? You mean that?"

"Not me, of course. Or this bunch," Carlos said, gesturing to our neighbors at the bar. "But to the voters."

"I'm not *that* weird … am I?"

"It's politics, *ese*. Perception. Anyway, you ran a good race. People respect that. I'll help you more next time."

"I need to get back to the Rotunda. I am not up here like you all. *Constantly,* that is."

"Thanks for the drink," Carlos answered. Others in the vicinity nodded.

"No problem. *O'Griego*."

"Black Irish, friend."

21

Speaking of money, the whole campaign exercise took a lot out of me, honestly. As a *professional* fund-raiser, I was supposed to have an edge that way, accustomed as I am to be asking for money. The truth of the matter is that I am a bit skewed in this area, coming as I do from money. Upon receiving a five-hundred-dollar donation for Hope House, for example, I would project enthusiasm, but inside I would truly expect another zero on that check. What are these donations except the best route to finally acknowledge that generosity is our only chance? While I might personally lend money to heroin addicts, even the most buttoned-up donor should be offended at the notion of "responsible philanthropy," in my opinion—an expression I swear I heard more than once at one of those stupid banquets where the kings and queens of local commerce congratulate themselves repeatedly. It is a hidden fury that animates me, and it certainly has made me an aggressive Development Director. All on behalf of Hope House.

But raising money for my own election, for my own political ambition? This was a different matter. Especially as my unpaid balance to my highly regarded campaign team began to escalate. I suppose it kind of snuck up on me, the expense I was actually incurring, as what I really wanted to do was simply to walk the neighborhoods; as campaign professionals they certainly supported that strange inclination of mine, but it soon became apparent that I needed to do some events, make some calls, ask individual donors. Phone time. Groan. I certainly was familiar with this kind of process but having it *all about me* instead of Hope House just felt wrong.

But as any political operative will admit, fund-raising is a measure of your viability. I came up with the idea of a St. Patrick's Day Party, early in the campaign season, before my time with the professionals really kicked in. Fifty dollars a person, where I would announce my candidacy. It ended up being primarily my basketball homies with their wives or girlfriends and primarily an excuse to drink dark beer. There were serious ward chairmen and retired schoolteachers in attendance as well—along with at least one state legislator—but it was mostly music, featuring my newly found disco globe, and lots of joking around. I do not think I gave a speech—other than a *thank you for coming*—and I could not help but catch the state legislator's attitude towards all of this frivolity. Emily assured me it went fine, and we did clear nearly one thousand on the event. The problem was, I needed much more than that—one thousand multiplied by seventy, eighty, even more. Once again, I was back asking people for money. Some readily gave, as puzzling as *that* was to me, as I have mentioned, no donation slip involved. But others wanted to be courted, which got me into certain situations that at this point in my life I should know how to navigate.

"It's all about self-interest," Grogan said, as if I were twelve years old. The waiter was taking unusually long. "Do you understand that?"

"Yeah," I answered, almost defensively. "Of course."

"Then why haven't you asked me what *my* interest is in your candidacy?"

"Well," I replied, "I know that you're a Democrat. And you live in my district."

Grogan laughed. "I just out-of-the-blue *appear* in your life and give you … how much so far?"

"You have been very generous. But Hope House is different, much more worthy, of course." The bottle of wine arrived, and Grogan nodded, after tasting. "I am in this whole other realm now."

"This is an excellent vintage, don't you think?"

"Yes. Definitely."

"You like that word, don't you? *Definitely.*" His eyes narrowed. Overweight, dyed hair, not a happy guy. "What is so *definite* about everything?"

"It's just an expression," I answered, unsure of where he was going. "I guess I'm passionate about things. I don't know …."

"I don't mean to criticize you. It's just something I notice. Along with the fact that every time we meet up, it ends up costing me. Three thousand two hundred and fifty-five dollars, to be exact."

"I really appreciate it," I said gamely. "I want to cover dinner, if you'll let me?"

"Oh, that's *great,*" he laughed. "I really make out with this arrangement."

"Well, what's *your* interest?" I asked him. Grogan smiled mischievously. "Politically, I mean?"

"Oh, that—good move there."

"We've been through the other thing," I answered, trying to keep it all on the objective plane. "You just have to believe that I enjoy your company. I value my male friendships."

"You would be *so* welcome in certain quarters."

"I am flattered by that. Truly."

"How is Emily?" he asked. "Does she know that we're out tonight?"

I restrained my urge to clarify to Grogan that this was not a date. "We're doing fine," I said instead. "And I was going to tell her about our meeting when I get home. Call her, I mean." People are just lonely. Grogan means well, I reminded myself. And he's a Democrat.

"Well, give her my best."

"I will."

"Can I make a toast?"

"Sure," I answered, raising my glass.

"To the successful candidacy of Chapman Murphy in District 10."

"Here, here."

"Where are you right now?" Grogan loved those double meanings.

"In the poll, you mean?"

"Yes." He nodded wearily. "The poll."

"We haven't run it yet. They are putting it together right now." I wanted to mention the high cost of these polls but thought better of it.

"She's going to be hard to unseat."

"I know."

"But if you get help from the top, on the national level ... I just have questions about his campaign. Democrats lose on the national level. Too often."

"I know."

"I've given them a lot of money," Grogan said angrily, his face beginning to redden. "I'm a businessman. We expect results. The other side understands that."

"What *is* your interest?"

"I was going to get to that," he shot back. Almost on cue, our main courses arrived.

"This is a nice place," I said. "I didn't know it was here."

"I'll get the owner to come by, if you want."

"No, that's okay."

"How's your steak?" he asked. "Is it cooked to your satisfaction?"

"Definitely," I replied, in between bites. "Okay, okay," I added. "I'll look at my phraseology."

"No, you're charming the way you are. Don't change."

"Hey, I'm always open for feedback."

"Are you familiar with the concept of 'collaborative entrepreneurship'?" he asked.

"Is that the same thing as 'multi-level marketing'? The pyramid thing?" He was not amused. "Okay, I was kidding. Tell me about it. It sounds good."

"I can spare you the details. That can wait. Except to say that when you're elected, I will expect certain behavior from you in return."

"Well," I answered, "I need to be educated on the issue, of course."

"Oh, I will *educate* you."

"Okay then. How's *your* steak?"

"Not as good as it could be."

"Still, it's a good place here," I said, looking at the velvet curtains, trying to ignore their romantic implications. We were seated next to each other, close.

"You must bring Emily here some time," he said, possibly reading my thoughts, "and tell her I suggested it."

"I will … do that."

Grogan allowed me to pick up the hefty check, and we went our separate ways, after our super-masculine handshake. Later that evening, Emily and I got into one of our volatile phone conversations:

"It was *not* a date," I protested vehemently.

"To him it was," she replied.

"Look, my work puts me in certain situations. And this running for office is ridiculous that way."

"I'm not jealous," she answered. "Except that I want you to understand that, with you, it's both the women and the men. Who you flirt with and such."

"Oh, please," I protested again. "Not true. That's a distortion."

"No, it isn't," she replied. "But I understand where it comes from."

"How patronizing."

"You just need to be honest with yourself," she continued, "about your behaviors."

"Look," I said with finality into the phone, "I don't want to discuss this now. I need to sleep. I have two appearances tomorrow. And God knows what else."

"I told you this would be hard for us," she answered.

"Just bear with me. The whole thing will be over soon."

There was silence on her end. A bit prophetic.

23

The residents at Hope House are living proof that loss can be overcome, and their vivid tales of botched operations and bad initiations and overall deprivation certainly put my own disappointments into perspective. I was not lit on fire by my father. I was not beaten by my cousin. I did not have an alcoholic uncle who lived in an abandoned car in the backyard. And so on.

But there is one resident who has actually become my best friend, in the normal sense of the word.

It was early in our programmatic history when I met Donald, and he straight up has the best laugh I have ever heard from anyone. A tall, beefy black guy he is (well, not that beefy), and everybody loves him—staff, volunteers, other residents. He was a Hope House resident forever—I think he still owns the record for length of stay in our program, along with the average pounds gained per month for a resident. (We figured it out once with a calculator, 4.5 a month.) To this day, I do not understand what led him into the crime he committed, as he had never been in trouble with the law. He was simply tired of being nice, he confided to me one evening, in between putts at the miniature golf course where we would often go on our programmatic outings. And he wanted to make a statement that he was not that nice a person. *Of course,* the gun was not loaded, and I can see

Donald apologizing profusely to the nice young bank teller. And then his *escape* plan was hardly that. He basically went back to military housing and waited for the authorities to come.

"Hey, dawg." It was Donald with his signature expression. I remember pulling up in the hotel parking lot where we worked.

"Shall I address you as 'supervisor' now?" I teased. "Is it true that you are running this place now?"

"This guy, the owner, he *trusts* me," Donald answered modestly.

"You are doing all of the hiring?"

"I guess."

"Not bad. Your parole officer must be impressed. I know that we are impressed."

"The owner, he's a good guy. He starts telling me all this information that I don't necessarily want to hear—you know, of a personal nature. About his marriage."

"Really?"

"Yeah," he laughed that laugh. "He just doesn't have anyone else to talk to."

"Well, does that mean that you can hire our residents too? Carte blanche?"

Donald stepped back from my car—at that time a three-cylinder American one. "Dawg," he began, "you have got to take better care of your ride." He was looking at its dusty outside. "When was the last time you had the oil changed?"

"Not *that* long ago."

"No wonder you have the board all nervous and whatnot."

"Why? Did somebody tell you something?"

"No," he lied. "But here you are, *Development Director* and whatnot, and driving around in a raggedy car." He paused. "And what is all that in the back seat?"

"Look," I said, "I don't make that much money. And this is a nice car."

"I could do some work on it for you."

"Just like the jet engines? In the Navy, I mean?"

"Man," he replied, "those things are *hard,* dawg. Real complicated." He was wearing those prison-issued black frame glasses, and they hung awkwardly on his nose.

"It's nice of you to offer," I replied. "But I'd rather you spend your energy on yourself. And on the hiring of our residents. We've got two new women coming in next week." This was back in the time that Colter loved to invoke, when we truly were the Hope Hookup House.

"Dawg," he answered, "that gets complex. Our ladies can be … you know, with what happened to them in childhood and all? Nobody is talking to each other right now, our two ladies from the house. Either here, or when we all go back for dinner. They're all mad—especially at me."

"What did you do?"

"Nothing!" he protested, flashing that grin of his. "I swear. It's just that Mr. Scott has entrusted me with this position, his wife being in rehab and all. And I owe it to him to get these rooms clean, as best I can. For him and our guests."

"They are not working out? Charlayne and Mary Lou?"

"They *hate* each other," he said with a laugh. "They come to me with what the other did. It's stressing me out. I'm starting to get gray, like you are."

"I don't have any gray hair. I mean, significantly." I looked in the car mirror for confirmation.

"All I know is that when you interviewed me and Jackson at minimum that day, you didn't have any. You looked seventeen, with your clipboard and all. And tennis shoes, no less."

"Well, anyway … I realize that you can't hire everyone."

"It's just these two, they drive me crazy. Because then they go from here to the house. Where we all live. I think they even have the same parole officer."

"Okay, we can work on that. We should probably bring it up at house meeting. I should probably go now."

"At least get your damned car cleaned. And stop wearing those tennis shoes."

"Okay, when you stop wearing those stupid glasses. Come on, man. You are in the free world now."

"I like my glasses."

"And I like my tennis shoes. They are actually of high quality."

"Fine," he answered. "See you back at the house."

This was early in our program, when monthly its survival seemed to hang in the balance. Though I suppose you could say that now as well. Drama in the house, drama on the board, and local parole regarding us as naïve do-gooders. Plus, always the *rumors*. Part of the reason Donald was with us so long was on account of our staffing instability: I would watch them come and go, the persons hired to preside over our colorful operation, but always the *personal* issues would assert themselves, and it was time for another ad in the paper. We joked at the time that we should institute a kind of cattle prod test: zap an applicant during the interview, full voltage, and if the zappee pretended it was not happening, then we could move on to the next one. This was all before Macey appeared, of course. But that group of Donald's was with us through it all—provided the only stability, really—and Donald was their reluctant leader. If I ever do get married, I will ask him to be my best man.

Anyway, I bring it up primarily because I often think of what he said once about the sadness of the world. He said something to the effect that people will revert, always, to the inertia of their aspiration. Something like that. And he told me how, as a child, he used to sit alone in his room, behind the window curtain, and how he would try to "catch the world in a lie," periodically peeking out. Donald did three years inside, then roughly two with us, and then he was quick to put that chapter of his life behind him. Someday maybe we could get him a pardon.

I am realizing now that I could have really benefited from his advice, his wise presence, during my campaign. But I was too busy at the time to see the obvious need to simply call him up and ask to him to resurface in my world. He could have told my campaign team what I was really about, deep down, which was something that I apparently had trouble conveying to them, at least early on, in those critical first few months. He would not have allowed me to misrepresent or embellish at all, Libra that he was. He would not have let them whiten my teeth like that in the photo—or at least he would have teased me about it. He would say that its fake quality would ultimately become symbolic for my whole campaign, and that the voters would sense it and whatnot. I could have been able to tell Emily that I did not need a therapist because a person does not have to pay someone like Donald for honest feedback. And what he said about the sadness in the world has stayed with me, along with the memory of his somewhat stooped and reluctant gait. I should have called him—still can—but I have learned that some of our residents do better with Hope House in their rearview mirror.

24

Emily is fabulous with her thick curly hair and green eyes and full lips and the way she fits into *all* of the clothes that I buy for her—petite, size two—and we did have fun hitting those stores together. It might seem odd that I should be in this role, given how fiercely independent she is; but to the degree that she was the artist and I was the politician, it made sense. Couples develop their rituals, and we had ours: clothing stores (the mirrored dressing rooms presenting certain possibilities), overnights at our respective places, bars where she would watch me drink, and *lots* of conversation. The thing about Emily is that she had no money at all, and with her slight pale form, it was as if she could float away at any moment. It was impossible for me not to feel protective of her, and livelihood was a huge issue for her. She got by, and was very creative at it, and her priorities were totally in the right place: painting; working with the troubled kids for a modest hourly rate; house sitting here and there.

When she called me that night, on her cell that would go in and out, on the starless mesa somewhere, her old Volvo barely functioning, I was concerned:

"Are you okay?" I asked nervously. "Where *are* you?"

"I am not sure where I am … somewhere. But sweetie, you won't believe what I have in the car with me."

"What do you mean, *in the car?*"

"It was the oddest thing. … I rounded this curve, and there was this very large form in front of me. On the highway, right in the middle. Guess what it was."

"I have no idea. Are you sure you're okay? Did you have a wreck or something?"

"Not at all. It was an owl. And it's in the back seat right now."

"What?"

"It was wounded, in the middle of the road, its wing, hopping around. I was afraid it would get run over. I caught it and put it in this basket that I just happen to have. It's here with me now."

"Are you serious?"

"Yes" she answered, her voice fading in and out on the phone.

"There's no traffic out there? Where *are* you?"

"I don't know," she answered. "Like I said. Somewhere near Madrid. I have a client out there, a poor troubled boy."

"Listen, that owl has talons, okay? Can you *please* make sure that it stays in that basket or whatever you have? Does it have a lid?"

"Yes. And it seems to be kind of sleeping right now. What should I do?"

"I don't know. Have no idea, really. … Except that I am very impressed. And very worried. At the same time."

"I called Sissy, and she suggested that I take it to this great animal shelter up the way. She checked it out. They specialize in wild animals."

"Which is what that thing is, okay? Please be careful."

"Okay."

This kind of situation was typical of what Emily brought into my conventional world, which, let the minutes reflect, I never thought was *that* conventional. At least before meeting her. There was so much about her that was almost feral, like that owl in her Volvo. I suppose she did raise herself in many ways, especially after her family lost the farm in such a public way. She was quick, and a survivor, but she did get depressed. Very depressed. Low energy dis-associative, would not eat. Hence the therapist, who apparently was not my advocate. And her psychotropic medication, which continued to be an issue between us.

25

I know that I project wildly onto Carlos, investing him with qualities that he probably does not possess. But especially after my desert island dream—the one where he is all wounded himself and sagacious in his empathy—he seemed like as good a confidant as any. But I certainly see how this projection business can work: I would get that myself during the campaign, for instance, with the doctored photo of my pearly white teeth. I would get these calls, with some gravel-voiced elderly man on the other end, relieved probably that I did not pick up: "I just wanted you to know," one guy said, "that I voted for *you*. And our Republican President." Or with the earnest and progressive bunch, after my quick five-minute appearance before them. By then I was losing my patience for nuance—a simple yes, no, yes. And maybe a curt but impassioned few words of elaboration, and me unclear on exactly who these people were and whether there was the *real* prospect of campaign. But feel free to project onto me whatever it is you wish to see. There were contributions at stake. And then the call shortly afterwards from their committee chair: "We wanted you to know that you were the best of all the candidates that we spoke with. We find your candidacy exciting and will be sending a check within a few days. We need more Democrats like you who will not back down from the vested interests."

And here is where I go dim. By default, I guess—am I that kind of Democrat? The political dialogue being extreme and stunted. Indeed, why bother with nuance? I had given simple answers: No, we should not pave over the ancient monuments for the sake of relieving traffic congestion. Of course, people of the same sex should be able to marry. And of course, government has no business dictating what a woman should do with her body.

All of the above made me a Progressive Democrat. Especially odd because I learned the darker lessons from my Republican father extremely well: the *oh, please, do we really need government to do that?* Let the free market work its magic. People need to take responsibility for their own choices. A person can be anything they want to be in this great country. Bootstraps. All of this very familiar to me, as Mike Powell is quick to point out. But that camp lost me, especially with *their* definitions being so skewed, so extreme.

Which is why I am both perplexed and baffled by the cordial if not delightful opposition—Mike, my worthy opponent, my dad, all of the shut-down guys that I play basketball with, including the occasional minister who tries to convert me in between games. What is it about them all? Bristling at intellect, a contagious *no,* and yet this penchant for their own brand of idealism? Somewhere in there I suspect a broken dream, a disappointment, the resulting trajectory towards cynicism, urged on, of course, by *that channel.* How they hate to be told that they are uncaring: if only we could appreciate the marketplace that will solve everything if given a chance. And then, of course, some quick reason for not being anyone's sap—the cheaters and malingerers, once exposed—and then they can therefore justify literally everything, as they can always point to these occasional freakish examples for proof of their viewpoint. We must not deny who we are, deep down. Anything but *government,* pronounced with sufficient derision, as history will teach us.

With his cutting deadpan, Mike Powell would say that it all comes down to individual choice. My attractive opponent would phrase it in terms of realism, that virtue cannot be *legislated*. My dad would have been offended by any comparison of him and Old Man Potter, and rightly so, his own narrative the product of a Depression-era childhood. And in my own family I learned what to *avoid* in my conversation. And that one completely polarizing issue—who is responsible for injecting *that* into politics? As we brighten with rage on both sides, the middle or in-between a disappearing fantasy? And now we have the rule of the grinning boys.

26

"Chapman," Colter said in a scolding tone. "When are you going to fix this car? Or at least get a new one?"

"Just lay off my car, okay? It's American, goddamnit."

"That's not the point," she answered. "God, you're weird."

"You two okay back there?" I asked, looking at Cesare and Colter.

"We're good," Cesare answered. "Sorry about the door. Handle is broken, I guess."

"Just drive us," Colter teased. "The Hope House chauffeur."

"Anything for the cause," I replied.

"So," Cesare began, "is this the same deal as last time?"

"Sort of," I answered. "Except that we are not presenting before a committee. We will first check in with Senator Cohen, of course. Then we are just going to walk around, remind certain members of how important our appropriation is. I'll have you back for dinner. At your respective houses, of course."

"That's not fun," Colter answered. "Can't we go out or something?"

"No. Your travel passes are very clear on that. Plus, it sucks when volunteers come over with dinner and no one is there."

"How much are we asking for?" Colter asked.

"Two hundred thousand dollars. "

"You sure that's enough?" she kidded.

"Look, you'd be surprised. By what is involved in tending to you people."

"Can they just cut us a check if it goes through?"

"In a way. First, we get into Senate Bill 2. Then the language invokes an emergency clause."

"Seems complicated."

"It has to be that way," I continued. "The state can't just issue us a check—it needs to be clear on what services it gets in return. Then they do an RFP, for a program suspiciously resembling ours."

"Oh."

"Keep this in the car, okay?" I continued. "But we are in trouble financially. We missed out on a couple of grants we were counting on. And Macey is good at that. Remember, we are a private charity."

"Let's do another raffle!" Colter interjected.

"We will. In due time. But we have to pay the bills in the meantime."

"I heard you ran for office." Colter continued. "Like, what kind of thing was that about?"

"State Senate. But I lost."

"I heard it was close," she replied.

"Depends on what you define as close. I don't think it was *that* close. But for a Democrat in this past election I did all right. At least, that's the perception."

"I still don't get this Democrat/Republican stuff," Cesare commented, staring out the car window. "Why can't you just run as who you are?"

"Because that's the way it's set up," I replied. "But people do run as Independents. They just tend to lose."

"Well, you lost anyway," he answered. "*A la ve?* Next time get me involved. I'll get the streets in your corner."

"The streets don't vote."

"No, for reals."

"Great. Then you'll just frighten everyone—not you personally, of course. Door to door with your clique."

"I'm not into that lifestyle anymore," Cesare answered quietly. "I know legitimate people. I've got family in your district, by the way. Cousins, I think. They need to know about you, *ese.*"

"Why don't you switch parties?" Colter asked innocently enough. "Sounds like you can't win with that one you're in."

"Don't tell me you're one of *them!*"

"I'm not anything. Hell, I can't even vote."

"Yes, you can. They changed that. When your parole is finished."

"All right, then," she laughed. "That's good to know. My problems will be solved now."

"It's just something that you might want to do," I said. "It being part of a normal life and all."

"I think the Republicans have some good ideas," she answered. "I hear them talk at my church."

"They *so* don't care about you," I answered. "Believe me."

"We shouldn't kill babies like that."

"Oh, *please,*" I replied. "Can we change the subject?"

"I believe in Jesus," she added.

"Good," I answered. "I'm glad that works for you."

"It was tough," she continued pensively, "the place I got into."

"I know, Colter." I found her eyes in the mirror. "Seriously, if that helped bring you back, *great.*"

"It was afterwards. Like when I realized that I had survived … it has to come from somewhere."

"Which party has the money?" Cesare asked.

"They both do, really. But the other side has bigger donors. Thank you both for doing this, by the way."

"It's the least we can do, Chappie," Colter replied, beginning to tear up. "Now put some decent music on. Not this new-agey stuff."

After protesting Colter's description of my favored music, we settled into a quiet ride to Santa Fe. We found a parking place near the west entrance, bumper-stickers from both sides being generously represented. Despite the turbulence of their respective pasts, both of my companions grew wide-eyed once again as we cruised the Rotunda, introductions being made in the random manner in which they presented themselves. Leading the way, I took them downstairs, where both chambers were in full representation, working to hammer out the specifics of government in thirty-one days. It was a short session. We were still not in the budget, according to my sources, but someone had spotted a potential two-hundred-thousand-dollar line item in the Corrections Budget, which was definitely encouraging.

The sergeant-at-arms hesitated when I gave him my card requesting the presence of Senator Cohen, eyeing my companions with uncertainty—I had forgotten about the tattoos and only saw how well-dressed they both were. I assured the sergeant that we would remain there, quietly, on the appropriate side of the line. He seemed satisfied, then came back quickly with the news that she could not see us now, that an important vote was approaching, but not to leave the building until we checked in with her. I thanked him, received my card back, and then we went topside to visit certain offices with our message of rehabilitation. I saw Carlos from a distance, but he looked busy. Then we ran into Mike Powell, who is a Hope House board member, and he graciously asked Cesare and Colter a couple of questions: how they were doing, where they were employed, et cetera.

And then he politely excused himself, off to champion his various bad causes.

"Hi there, Senator," I began, in an attempt at humor. It was her, the incumbent I had tried to unseat.

"You picked a good time," she answered, without sarcasm. "Five minutes ago, I was giving a speech."

"About what hateful subject?" I smiled to let her know I was kidding.

"Please," she smiled. "It's not my fault that you are in the wrong party."

"You mean the one you used to be in?"

"That was then," she answered. "This is now. I saw the light. What can I say?"

"Does anyone ever give you a hard time about that? Seriously. I mean your Pueblo is hardly a Republican fortress."

"My tribe understands that I work on their behalf. I just happen to be a Republican."

"I thought we had you there for a while."

"You ran a good race," she replied. "Except for those mailings."

"What about *your* mailings? Sorry that I didn't go to Yale. I just attended that loser college Brown."

"And where did you get that photo of me?" she replied. "The one that you chopped up. And calling me a liar?"

"Sorry about that. If it was up to me, we would not have done that."

"Weren't you the candidate?"

"You know how it is," I continued. "I actually wanted to call and warn you, but at that point, the wheels were in motion. … You know that you have beautiful hair?"

"Thanks," she answered, slightly blushing. "I guess …"

"I just always wanted to tell you that."

"So, what brings you up here today? Anything I can help you with? After all, you are my constituent. Even if you tried to take my job."

"Hope House. The usual. We need to be in that budget. We've got some cash flow issues."

"Maybe if you hadn't chosen to run against me. I assume you took a leave of absence?" I nodded. "Then your fund-raising must have suffered."

"We didn't get a couple of grants. That really threw us off."

"But of course, I'll do what I can. Even though you're probably plotting right now to run against me. Again."

"You beat me. It was not really close."

"It was closer than we thought it would be. … I like Hope House. I always have. I'll talk to my side."

"Thanks."

On the notion of running again, I do have a persistent streak. As my mother used to say, *anything worth doing is worth doing well.* But if you are going to go through all of that effort to compete, it would be nice to win. The problem is the way District 10 is constructed—or shall I say strategically shaped? During the redistricting session, my side was not paying enough attention to the imminent future of a certain swath of Precinct 315, which seemed to be innocuous vacant land at the time. The crafty Republicans, however, knew that it would soon be developed into high-end homes, which had certain partisan implications. My friend Mike Powell knew exactly what he was doing. And certainly, that was my revelation when I ventured up to the Bluffs in midsummer and encountered a growing Republican stronghold that did not exist several years back.

Also, it was kind of weird when I would go to my campaign consulting firm's office, in an old brick building next to the railroad tracks. They had no idea what the sound of rumbling freight trains evoked in me, as we never really went too far back into my past. I suppose that I have always inhabited wildly different worlds, but it did feel rather schizophrenic at the time. But the experience of going door to door was uplifting, on balance; people on their best behavior, mostly, flattered at the notion of an early-afternoon visitor. Our conversations rarely progressed beyond the pleasantries, and I was not good at hammering home my robotic, consultant-dictated message, the buzz phrases that my campaign manager wanted me to repeat. *We need new faces up there, new energy. For the new day, the path to a brighter tomorrow…* and so on. Instead I usually ended up talking about sports, or where their kids went to school, or where I was originally from, or even the weather. I grew up in rural Iowa, this was all familiar to me, and I was raised to be polite. On a deeper level, my parents had instilled in me an abiding respect for people, no matter what their economic status was, or what their choices in life were. I must have been making some headway on the electoral front, as our polling indicated that I was getting closer and closer.

And I enjoyed it.

27

That one bad channel, blaring away constantly in certain people's homes. What is it? The tone, so *with us* it can render us speechless in protest. Modulations of indignation that build in ferocity. The call-in shows alive with personal disappointments, a collective daily catalogue of complaint, to be repeated at the same time tomorrow. Thinking back, I recognized it for maybe the first time in the basement den of that fraternity that I did not belong to, the game commentary loud and the beer flowing. People beginning to take liberties with their conversation, as if we were all of one mind on *those people*—a black face inviting ridicule on the screen. The *comments* and the coarse laughter, and I was supposed to follow along because we were all white boys in the basement, getting drunk in between exams. It was all part of my initiation into the larger world, those moments that would extend into the following years, always foreign to my small-town upbringing, where the goodness of people was the main theme. The soft Iowa evenings after practice. And now, decades later, an entire culture warming themselves around the morning radio with their bitterness. Can you believe the mother deserting her kids like that? Can you fathom that he was actually on parole at the time of his crimes? Is it possible that *this* could be happening here in our great nation? Or that our Allies across the Atlantic would *turn* on us, after all we have done for them? The French. And my friends like Mike Powell went about furthering this theme that seems to be gaining control—their majority in both national chambers. Except here, in our state—the land of Carlos, O'Rourke, Santiago, and my sad ex-felons.

"Chapman," Colter began, as we settled into our return trip, "if we don't get the money this time ... then there's something wrong."

"There's plenty wrong," I replied. "Like in the world and stuff. We're just fortunate to be in this position."

"But everyone wants us to have it!" she protested. "Like your wacko liberals and the other guys with the cowboy hats."

"It's a citizen's legislature, that it is." I replied. "But *none* of this is easy."

"What do you mean by *liberal?*" Cesare asked, a serious expression on his face. Colter and I looked at him. "No, really. I don't know what any of this means."

"Neither do I," I replied.

"The liberals are the ones who come and cook at the house," Colter began. "They are all caring and like that."

"We have conservative volunteers as well," I corrected her. "You'd be surprised."

"What's wrong with being a liberal?" Cesare asked Colter. "You say it like it's a bad thing."

"It's just …" I interjected, "that liberals have suffered some losses in recent years. There's a natural reluctance to be identified with them."

"They're like, losers," Colter interrupted. "*Ese* Cesare?"

"And the point is to win," I added.

"Damn," Cesare laughed. "This stuff is whacked. But I like it. … Do you think that I could end up there some day?" he asked, directing his attention towards me in the mirror.

"Who knows?" I answered in a positive tone. "Go to school and see what happens."

"Yeah," Colter echoed. "Now that we can vote."

"After you successfully complete your parole."

"No problem," Cesare answered softly. "I want to make something out of my life. I think I know some things."

"I'm just glad neither one of you absconded," I said, smiling. "You had your chance. With those travel passes of yours."

"And what would we be escaping into?" Colter replied.

Which was the whole point. On many levels. But I kept quiet.

28

I should mention at this point that I have worked out an escape plan if we do not get the funding from the Legislature: one thing I learned from my deceased father is to *always keep your options open.* I do not mean to be dramatic; in fact, I hate it when people do that. I have to simply acknowledge that I am in *way* over my head, on numerous fronts. I know that I should just stay put and *work* on these things as grownups do, but things have happened that make it impossible for me to grow up in a standard fashion. I have no idea how I will exit—the specifics I mean—but exit I will. The hardest thing would be my relationship with Emily—though I suspect she will clearly beat me to that particular juncture, the way things have been going. Still, I had hoped that I could somehow move into a simpler way of being with her. I had certainly learned much in my relationship with Kit. But there seemed to be a pattern in both with me not meeting certain expectations. I do feel capable of delivering on that front, let the minutes reflect; Colter's teasing about me never being able to escape bachelordom is simply not correct. I have things that I want to accomplish—like winning that red license plate.

With Emily, the promise of our connection can be problematic, as I really do need to get off the phone and return to work, much to her frustration. And I seem to have an unending appetite for solitude, and there is always enough time in a day, or night, to claim that. Give me what I need in that respect, I say: errands invented, lofty thoughts pursued, and of course the television awaits with its array of channels (except the bad one). Something happened to me as a kid to make me like this, which of course I *realize* and do not need Emily to continually point out. And yes, it does matter—these specifics of childhood—but I do not need to hire somebody to go excavating with their headlamp. I have my suspicions about what it is, if pressed, and could hear it from someone other than a relational partner. But, as a friend says, we repress things for a reason: it serves an invaluable function that way. So that we can proceed with our lives and all of that.

With my plan of escape, I have narrowed it down between the Greyhound and another option that I do not want to talk about right now. Again, I don't mean to be dramatic, but futility can take its toll if a person just looks around—the houses and the children, the less than ideal private circumstances, the accumulating number of messages on my cell that I cannot bring myself to return. I ran my race and now can add that to the list of unsuccessful attempts at belonging. There is still one of my signs out there off the highway, withering in the rain. Hope House would at least be missed if it folded—Cesare, Colter, Donald, even—we have definitely had a nice run. And it is not like the need will ever go away. If the funding runs out it won't be totally our fault, as we definitely tried. And everyone understands that the charitable sector endures fluctuations; the casual observer might even say that it was remarkable that we got it up and running in the first place: we would like to *start a halfway house in your neighborhood. Do you mind?*

I keep all of this mostly to myself, for many good reasons. And I actually ran for political office, on top of all this? You have got to be kidding. Better probably that I was defeated. One thing that I have learned over the many years of asking people for money is the importance of restraint: we all have our burdens, and what point is there in turning the spotlight on yourself? My job has been to listen, and I think that I have done that well. Trotting merrily along, tending to the concerns of the beleaguered. Why dwell on it? It just takes over then, which is a downer by any definition.

29

I am still dazzled by the inlaid marble that spells out our incomprehensible state motto: *going as grows,* or something like that. And always I am entranced by the beauty of our demographics: the mariachi children and the powwow dancers and the 4-H Club from *that* part of the state. I had wanted to belong to this in a deeper way, to be officially on the other side of the line, as I have mentioned. Somehow, if I had won, the decisions of the past would have been validated. We all have certain potential, and who can say why some get there and others do not? I see it daily, even on the basketball court. It is just limited being a visitor, though it has its advantages, clearly. The special status of the stranger. I am not sure where this desire to be an elected began, its very root. Was it my stint at Iowa Boys State, where, as high school juniors, we explored the mysteries of simulated governmental office? And then there was my summer before college in D.C., as a Congressional Intern, for one of the most conservative House members even back then—after all, he did represent my rural Iowa district. He proved to be a reasonable fellow, though, and let us roam the Capitol halls at will, no being confined in a back office stuffing envelopes. Then at Brown I did win a seat in the University Senate, going door to door in a couple of dorms. And I did major in History, loved discussions about whether or not FDR saved democracy.

But then everything went dormant for a decade or two, as I faced the challenges of building an adult life. I was not a very good voter, being preoccupied with whatever I was interested in at the time, but I think I did vote in all presidential elections. But once in the Roundhouse, on that first day, on behalf of my beloved charity, my desire to be a recognized public official was instantly ignited. When the opportunity came, I took it.

"Hey, Murphy!" It was Joshua again. I do love these young political operatives, male and female, trolling the hallways in their be-suited ambition.

"What, is *everybody* up here today?" I answered. "Or is my world just constricting?"

"Shut up. We were just talking about your race this morning."

"I don't get it. I lost. It's that simple. My dad, when he was alive, never cared for post-mortems."

"Look," he replied, sort of excitedly, "your race had all of the emerging demographics in play. Voting behaviors. It's worth reviewing."

"Good. Then you can do that. Go right ahead." I paused. "It's the numbers, right?" I continued. "There's no way I could have won. Unless there was a different outcome at the top."

"That's not necessarily true." He hesitated, looking at my clipboard. "Where's your pile of business cards?"

"Out of plain sight."

"Good," he teased, "you worry me."

"You're not the only one."

"How's Emily?"

"Fine."

"She's beautiful. Have you set a date?"

"Come on. Who cares these days whether a person is married or not?"

"We care about you."

"Who's *we?* The party?"

"You should do it, dude. Before you lose her."

"If I choose to do so—if *we* choose to do so—it won't be for *political* reasons." I did not feel like going into the details of our recent troubles with this guy.

"Why not? It's as good a reason as any?"

"Tell me again how I'm a … *pragmatic progressive?*"

Joshua thought for a minute. "Okay. Start with the obvious part of you that couldn't care less."

"You mean my lack of ideology?"

"No. More your laziness—that we all share. Even the zealots in our camp. Deep down."

"I care more than I used to. And I definitely care about what I *care* about. If you know what I mean."

"But even in that case you don't care *that* much. What, are you going to *lose sleep* over whether or not the safe antifreeze measure passes?"

"No. But that's not a good example."

"All I'm saying is that all is forgiven over a pitcher of beer."

"I don't drink beer."

"You should."

"I used to."

"But you hang with the opposition? I've seen you."

"They are people, too. Just misguided. Plus, it's my job as an advocate. Both sides."

"Fine. My point is that you could lead with that aspect of your personality. Skeptical, result-oriented, not ideological."

"I am definitely the latter."

"I am just saying don't rule anything out. And get married."

"Sure thing, Joshua."

"You're weird," he said flatly. "But not too weird."

"Is that a compliment?"

"I think you could win that seat," he answered. Then he shook my hand. "I've gotta go." He was off as quickly as he had appeared.

I should mention at this point that I never used the word *tedious* until recently, and its current prevalence in my vocabulary has me somewhat concerned. Thankfully, my work at Hope House keeps me from going too far down that road—Colter, for one, would not stand for it. Despite the accumulating years of service to my charity, there was always the renewal in a new motley crew of residents. The problem is, the routine can ring so *flat,* the daily chore of fund-raising, the daunting march towards solvency. The sales calls are hard: Donald used to marvel at my ability to persevere. People are mean, he would say, but they like to believe that they are not. That is where *you* come in, he would add. You give them a chance to prove themselves. Then they revert to their mean-spirited selves. Hoarding money. Pushing other people down the stairs. At this point, Donald would laugh his laugh. I would counter, of course, that people just need to be *educated* about the needs of the world around them, though I would acknowledge to him my own lack of patience in that regard. The zeroes did seem lacking, as I have mentioned, and the shabby donations of broken furniture and outdated weight machines got on my nerves. You expect too much, Donald would reply. Because you grew up rich. Hold on a minute, I would protest, my background has nothing to do with it. Then he would laugh and call me dawg and go back to his wizardry with the swamp cooler. He hooked everybody up.

For somebody who is supposed to be a carefree bachelor, I sure have a lot of responsibilities that keep me up at night: how on earth to raise all of that money that we need to stay open? The situation with Emily? How to make room and submit to the essential neighborhood meetings? I get tired, and I am not sure what to do. But when I have to cover dinner at the facility, to substitute for Macey—that one particular night recently an example of teamwork—the likes of Cesare or Colter or numerous others with *real* concerns pull me back on track. Their lives are broken, the cumulative years of incarceration have had their effect; it is the only place in my life where human fallibility has been acknowledged, and it frees me from my *own* prison.

The currents that do actually work for me at this juncture are simple and barely functional: Hope House, my political interest, and Emily. I am not big on class reunions; and when people do surface from my past, I am polite but kind of blank as to their importance. In the case of my brothers and my by now numerous nephews and nieces, I really do wish them well, as their lives move steadily away. I am baffled by this, I have to say, but I left years ago—I had my reasons—which maybe I should talk about, but I would rather drink cappuccino and run through the hit list of prospects that could actually help us through our two-hundred-thousand-dollar problem. Still, as isolated as I might be from my family, that did not keep them from following my election night online—and a pair of very nice phone messages ensued, messages that I did not erase.

"What is *up?*" I said to Santiago, extending my hand. "Remember me?"

"Of course, I remember you," he replied, looking slightly bleary-eyed, maybe from the previous night. "You're like my therapist."

"I'm just older than you, guy. And it runs both ways, *ese.*"

"That's good—especially for a *huero.* You'll have to come up north with me sometime. After the session."

"There is no life after the session."

"This is not a life," he answered. "This is an artificial existence."

"Are you behaving yourself?" I asked him gently.
"I *want* to. My girl is sweet, don't you think? You met her, right?"

"Yes. On both counts."

"How about Emily? Is that her name?"

"Same situation, guy. I would be an idiot to lose her. Plus, I am older than you."

"You keep saying that. But you don't look it."

"It's there if you actually look, rest assured. I feel *centuries* older than you. I guarantee it. Wandering pathless in the mountain range of my feelings and all of that."

"Whatever. You're sticking around tonight?"

"Should I?"

"There's always something," Santiago shrugged. "The machinery of government … how things get done."

"I should get home instead. For the sake of the *relationship.*"

"Yeah," he answered with attempted enthusiasm. "The *relationship.*"

"No, seriously, guy," I continued. "We can be better than we are. We should strive for that. As men, I mean."

"But we are beasts."

"That is not true. And you know it."

"Fucking *huero* Democrats."

"Later, guy," I said, extending my hand. "I'll be checking up on you."

30

The problem with what I do for a living is that there is always an agenda involved, even though we might pretend otherwise. And here I am talking about my role as Development Director for Hope House. I mean, I am interested in just about anyone, and I think I am good about asking questions. But I have grown tired of having to sit through all of their *stories,* before you get to the donor request. Or the more important stories when you have to at least issue a comment in response. Or the way that you have to sometimes pretend you are really hungry, as if you are not coming from a breakfast meeting very similar to this one (all of these *meals!).* Meanwhile, you are trying to figure out when is the best time to make the ask: do you get it out of the way in the beginning, for example, or do you wait like a silent tiger until dessert?

What a strange vocation, my livelihood; I rarely do it as I should, meaning it can take *weeks* before I am in the proper mood, the business cards and call lists languishing on my car dashboard. I suppose if I ever were to be elected to the Legislature, it would present a change on this livelihood issue. I would have to make some choices. Or at least my board would. My leave of absence during my candidacy experiment showed on our bottom line, as I have mentioned. Fund-raising is *hard,* as most of the time I want to be left alone, with my rituals that Emily is always commenting upon. I do not want to be faking an appetite at 12:30 in the afternoon, listening intently to some incomprehensible story of mortgages gone awry, or insurance boards issuing a directive. Here, too, Emily implies that my attention span is bad, that I *drift* around the room constantly, though I swear to her that I am not looking for intrigue. I probably do ingest way too much caffeine, but with this vocation of waiting it is hard to do otherwise. Still, I manage to pull it together when the checkbook is pulled out, and I have learned how important it is to keep quiet at that precise moment—when the decision is actually being made as to how much to give.

I was never any good at math, though, and truly, how else could I realistically think that we can make our annual budget on a consistent basis? I am always reassuring the board that we can do it—that we have untapped resources in the community—but then I am left to yet another fitful night of sleep, worrying. I *did* send out those personal solicitations a few months back, but of course they are going to be tossed out, even if I hand-addressed them and invoked our urgency. Our donors are besieged with these kinds of requests— always full of drama—and why should they be the only ones to shoulder society's burdens? They will ignore it unless I am persistent enough to call them personally, which on my end I would rather avoid.

31

Donald was somebody that I could just hang with, silently, as the world around us we both understood. The mall, the TV room at the facility, the church committees—always that color to it, inescapable, though perhaps buried in the laughter and fine conversation that passed between us. It was not like it was our *fault* or anything, or anyone else's. It was simply in the texture of the moment, the vibe in the room before we did our presentations, before the elderly social ministry committees. Then, on the way back to the facility, Donald would ask me again about our budget, where all the money was spent and so forth. I would defensively answer that staffing was important, that none of us was getting rich off the endeavor, but something in his Libra sensibility remained unconvinced. "You should just let it run on its own," I remember him saying. "Like one of those meetings my parole officer says I have to attend." It just does not work that way, I pointed out to him. It's like the difference between a one-hour meeting and three months together in the same house. Human nature being what it is. He nodded, then said: "It just would be cheaper, dawg. And you wouldn't be going gray like you are."

I know I have the wrong last name and all of that, but I love this state and the crazy political ambition that it elicits in me—I do not know how I got into this role out here, though, always asking strangers for money. No wonder that it has progressed to the point where people cross the street to avoid me or pretend not to see me at parties. Inevitably, it becomes a morale issue for me, whether we get the donation or not—there is just *so* much to raise. Still, I am certain that if I made my calls like I should, enough would shake loose, and of course, I owe it to Hope House to follow through. I do not know what is wrong with me sometimes. Even with my pals on the basketball court I am distant and removed, lazily hanging out in the sunny corner where I can best hit my three-pointer. Adonis let me have it the other day, in his patented harsh tone. "What are you *doing?*" he said furiously. "Get in the game! We need your shot, jerk." Like a lot of these guys, he is intensely competitive, and who wins these pickup games becomes a grave concern indeed. I mean, I care also, wanting to live up to our random team's collective potential and such. It is no fun to relinquish the court by losing. I just seem to draw a lot of comments, like I somehow become *symbolic* for their own individual issues. So, accordingly, I move to the *other* corner, where it is less sunny, and I redouble my effort to ask for the ball and take my guy off the dribble—just to keep Adonis and the others happy.

I go into this only because I want to convey what is important to me: after noontime basketball I just sit here, in my solitary office, doing nothing. My prospects at this point do not exactly return my phone calls or find my glib notes interesting, which is definitely fine with me. I should probably work more on my exit strategy, as who knows what will happen at the Legislature. Because I am back at work— no more charged pursuit of voters. I drink more cappuccino and hope for the best. Our state is not good on the per-capita income front, and the unfortunate few of impressively comfortable means are on every charity's list, including ours. I have lived with this reality for over a decade now, more than that—somehow, we have managed—but the bar keeps getting higher, as does our operational expense. At least, I dress like I am actually going to do some work: suit, tie, an outfit that evokes the Eastern Seaboard, apparently.

Emily goes on about seeing a therapist, but I am not a fan of her therapist, that's for sure; homie dishes out the meds like it's no big deal. And she is dis-associative enough. Hence the irony of her coming at me with that accusation, as she does constantly: "Where *are* you?" she will ask. "Right here," I will answer. "Right freakin' here." She talks about the importance of changing one's behavior, and I counter with the notion of simply doing that, changing it, bingo. She then objects vociferously, pointing out that the deeper reasons driving the behavior need to be examined. And I reply to her that it is an imperfect world, obviously, and who is paying attention anyway? Other than Adonis and the others who bark at me during noontime basketball.

And speaking of paying attention, our next move should be to make sure that the Governor knows the importance of this possible appropriation—with its emergency clause—if we are fortunate enough to be there at the end. As he is a recent Democratic standard-bearer, you would think it would be fine, but I never really know where I stand with him or his people. You really never know in this game. But he did say those very nice things about me that night at the Barela fund-raiser.

32

I really don't mean to go into postmortems about my unsuccessful bid for political office, but it was just a very intense experience for me. There was one guy, for example, who, I became convinced, would forecast whether I won or lost, as he had been visited by my opponent as well; whomever he chose would win, I reasoned.

"What do you want?" he asked gruffly upon opening his front door. He was an older fellow who clearly lived alone.

"I don't mean to disturb your pleasant evening," I began, handing him my flier. "But this is the political season. And people like me are out."

"I know," he said, regarding my glossy gift. "Your competition was here yesterday."

"She was?" I almost gasped. "It's been months now. And she hasn't walked at all. At least, to my knowledge."

"Well, like I said, she came by yesterday. With her kids. And those damned cats of hers."

"She was walking with her kids?"

"Yeah. And these cats. She was nice enough," he paused.

"You know I'm a Republican, right?"

"Yes, I do," I replied cheerily. "It says right here. We get these lists."

"But I always vote for the best person," he continued.

"Well, she didn't appreciate my language when her cats ran into my house. I told her, 'Get those goddamned things out of my house.'"

"Cats? She was walking with *cats?*" It was late afternoon, and I was getting punchy.

"Like I said. They just ran into my house. I don't think they peed anywhere, though."

"She got mad?" I asked.

"It was my language. Her kids were there. Is she religious?"

"I think so," I answered diplomatically.

"Well, she scurried out of here pretty quick. Why should I vote for you?"

"First of all, I'm a Democrat, but I want you to know that I come from a family of Republicans. It's not like I can't appreciate your viewpoint. I like working with people of different viewpoints. And, of course, I would bring that ability to the State Senate."

"What do you think about taxes? Democrats love to stick us that way."

"My dad was a successful businessman. I know how taxes can crush an entrepreneur."

"I'm retired," he laughed. "Well, I'm supposed to be. I've paid my fair share."

"Look," I continued, "Mr. Tippet?"

"That's the name. What else you got on there?" He squinted his eyes, looking at my clipboard.

"Oh, just that you are an independent-minded Republican."

"Okay."

"My message to you is this: if I'm elected, you will know who your State Senator is. Starting with this conversation. Most people in the district do not know who their senator is. It's rare for her to actually visit someone."

"Why did she pick me?"

"I don't know. This is an important precinct. We both want to do well here."

"I remember the fella that used to be in office. ... What was his name?"

"Senator Baca?"

"Yeah, that guy. He used to come by all the time. Nice fellow. I never voted for him, but he sure made the effort."

"Well, I would be *that* kind of senator. We can do better. Public schools. Health care. Crime. These are all important issues to our state. Taxes, like you say."

"I'll look it over," he said, surveying my flier.

"Will you keep me in mind?"

"I'll keep you in mind."

I love that phrase: *just keep me in mind.* Not too committal, but still asking for something from a relative stranger. I think I like to work so much because there is this instability waiting for me otherwise. On the weekends even, I am inclined to get out of bed quickly, as off to the office I go—always plenty of details demanding attention, or the high for a response to a well-timed email. During the week it is obvious too, as I will not return to my solitary home until after dark, as if twilight represents something foreboding in its potential. I should mention that I have always been this way—even back at Brown when I would not return home for Thanksgiving or even Christmas sometimes. Calm in the library stacks I would be gaining on the competition. Emily, oriented as she is towards asking questions, has naturally wondered what *this* is about. I keep telling her not to get offended, that it is only what keeps me going, but of course she counters with the notion that I am running away from something. I am careful not to leave too abruptly when she is staying over, but it must be obvious in my face that something is pacing inside. I do not know what to make of Emily and her questions: I guess I should be flattered, but I am usually irritated instead. Who knows why I expect so much from those closest to me—as if I am entitled to *instant* understanding simply by our shared presence.

It is not as if I experienced anything close to such a thing in my immediate family growing up. I was on my own at a young age, emotionally, though it did suit me for whatever reason. It was nothing personal with my parents or my brothers, just that they were having this family experience and I was not. It was easy to stop going home, well after the college days, as I would always want to interrupt the prized television shows with an attempt at conversation. Similarly, on the golf course or wherever these brothers of mine were assembled, as it seemed strange to talk about sports all the time, though I was as mad for athletics as anyone. Maybe *that* is how my political interest began, as at least we would get close to authentic speech in that arena, and we could all be conveniently removed enough not to get too fired up about our differing opinions. My father would go right up to the line in these heated discussions—something in my manner would almost tip him over—but then he would return to his drink and his nightly business report, my mother nervously concerned about possible dining room conflict. And my brothers did not really care about these distant matters anyway, as they asked to be excused for practice or homework.

It is absurd, really, any complaints that I might have about my upbringing. Especially in comparison to the lives I have known at Hope House. I have no problem being alone, and I guess that is a theme here. It is only recently that I have become aware of how odd it might seem to others, as once again I am solitary in the restaurant, surrounded by my newspapers. But tailored to campaigning I have become, ironically, as a weekend of knocking on the doors of a precinct—filling out both the mornings and the afternoons accordingly—is an embarrassingly easy fact. Emily would sometimes come along, slowing me down, of course, but it made for a healthier day; I realized soon that it helped me too, as voters were less inclined to wonder about this man plying their neighborhood. But of course, I did the bulk of it alone. For months.

"Hey, Murphy," I heard a man's soft voice from across the road. "Why don't you come over here in the shade?" It was a timely invitation, as I was starting to grow dizzy in the afternoon heat, and this was a particularly tricky neighborhood to cover—long, dirt driveways back into the trees, electronic gates serving their purpose, and dogs everywhere.

"That's nice of you," I called out to Loyola, having recognized him from the morning breakfast group, over the light traffic of the scenic boulevard. "I think I will."

"It's too hot to be walking," he said, his weathered face a snapshot of the Valley's history.

"But it's Saturday, guy. People are home." I crossed the road. He gestured to a lawn chair with his shaky hand. "You know that, right?" I continued. "From your days as Mayor."

"Oh, yeah," he nodded. "But back then, everybody knew everybody else. You knew who your neighbor was. It was a village back then. Separate from Albuquerque." There was a shakiness in his voice, and my math was good enough to place him in his mid-eighties. "Do you want some wine? I've got a vineyard out back. Pretty good crop this year."

"Sure," I said. "Why the hell not? Nobody's actually home anyway."

"I like your chances," he said, referring to my race.

"Really? Even though I'm not from here?"

"Aw, that's okay. You're Irish. That almost counts."

"You got any suggestions about how I can win this thing?"

"She's going to be tough." It was hard to know where to meet Loyola's gaze, as his unusual blue eyes were cloudy. But they were definitely alive and watching. "Just make yourself comfortable," he said, and then he moved into his well-maintained adobe, which I assumed had been there forever—in contrast to the new, surrounding estates, with their goddamned gates. His dog began to growl, which was disconcerting because of his breed and my recent bad luck in that area. "Don't mind Fuego," Loyola called out reassuringly. "He's all right. Fuego's a Democrat."

"Okay," I said in the pit bull's direction. "Nice doggie." Fuego seemed satisfied, finding his place under the tree, gnats following his course. Loyola then reemerged from his house with two plastic cups of red wine.

"Here you go, Senator." We toasted each other.

"I wish," I answered.

"It's a different district now, isn't it?" Loyola asked. "All the new houses."

"No kidding. And then with how far it goes up into the Bluffs," I answered. "And then across the river to the other side."

"You're going about it the right way, though. Walking like you are."

"That's the assumption." I took another sip. "This is *good*," I said, meaning it. "It's sweet—but not too much."

"It's been a pretty good year," Loyola repeated. "My wife and I planted these vines decades ago. She's no longer with me."

"I'm sorry."

"It will be fifteen years in August. I never thought I'd outlive her."

"Wow," I said, kind of awkwardly. "That's a long time."

"I promised her I'd keep going to Mass, though."

"I've seen you there. At Sacred Heart."

"You should get out more," he said pointedly. "I haven't seen *you* there. You're new here. Nobody knows you."

"That's why I'm walking," I said defensively, in spite of myself. I was starting to feel the wine.

"You should have gone to the fiestas, too."

"I know," I said, meaning it. "It's my campaign manager. He really pushes the walking and phoning. Direct voter contact. He's not big on parades, fiestas."

"I'm telling people to vote for you. The guy from Iowa. I have a cousin who lives there now."

"It's different in Iowa."

"That's what he says."

"Loyola, I really appreciate your support. Telling your friends and all."

"*Mi familia también*. Enough votes there that should help a little."

"Great."

"Senator Baca speaks highly of you. Says you do a good job up there in Santa Fe, even if you are new to the Valley."

"I want to have that chance. To be up there officially."

"It's not like it used to be," Loyola continued. "I don't know any of these families living next to me. Used to be nothing but alfalfa fields along the road here. And a few horse ranches."

"Did you like being Mayor of the village?"

"Oh yeah. It's not for everybody, is it?"

"No," I replied.

"You're good, though. People like you."

"It's just this Irish stuff or something. It kind of wells up in me from somewhere."

"I was telling my nephew yesterday," Loyola continued, "you can't have community without knowing who your neighbor is. Can you?"

"I don't think so. Like you say, everybody is off on their little island. Along *this* road, for example."

"It hurts us as Democrats," Loyola replied.

"Yeah," I answered. "Add that to the list." I gulped down the rest of the wine. "I gotta get going, guy. There are voters out there. Even if nobody's home."

"Okay. Stop on back. Bring some signs, too."

"I will. *Gracias*." We shook hands.

Why do I love this neighborhood so much? I mean, when I impulsively moved on the last possible day in order to pull this off, I really did have little idea about my new immediate surroundings. Carpetbagger. I certainly knew nothing about irrigation rights and land grants and what a rich political legacy I was elevating myself into. My first wakeup call was when Manuel called me out of the annual parade and asked me that question about who in the hell I was. Kind of unreal to think about it, that I actually *did* all of this. As with so much in my life, I guess I just did not know any better.

But certainly, in retrospect, I could not have *expected* these old families of this tight-knit community to rally behind me. Or at least vote in enough numbers to offset her advantage in the Bluffs. Especially the old guys, the *patrones*—like Loyola and Manuel and former Senator Baca and the guys at the restaurant—how quickly they welcomed me in. But then, being a Democrat made for a good start. Maybe that was all there was to it. The least I could do in return is speak Spanish, for Chrissakes; I had had enough of it in college, you would think. As the months went by, I did fall in love with this genuinely foreign world that I had stumbled into and wanted only to make it up to them by becoming their senator. I would be *devoted* to them and the district; I *would* be, if given the chance. I had tried to convey that in my endorsement interview with the paper—how public service is all I have in the familial sense—but they did not really understand it, I don't think. (That one guy looked really puzzled at what I was driving at.) Or at the very least I was asking the newspaper to consider my oddity status as a positive. But in the end, they concluded, *in print,* that I was fundamentally not in touch with the district, unlike my opponent, walking with her cats. No matter how many households I personally visited over the course of five months.

I did feel like a complete impostor, however, when I dragged Emily to Mass—at Sacred Heart of course—two weeks before Election Day. Manuel and the others smiled in recognition as they passed the collection basket around, and I did my best after the service to explain that this visit was not as tactical as it seemed. I mean, if I am going to put up billboards in their neighborhood and not even speak their language, the least I could do was attend Mass? And, in fairness to myself, I had been there on several other occasions, at the pulpit no less, relaying the Hope House story and hawking our raffle tickets with Colter and the others.

Still, my timing was inescapable, as was the concern we had about extremist leafleting. Fortunately, Father Maestas would have *none of that* in *his* parking lot, Jesus being impartial in these political matters.

33

I probably should not mention this, as we are a democracy and all of that, but I cannot believe how difficult it is to sit through some of these community political meetings. On the ward level, or the precinct level—the grassroots thing—and of course, everything is colored by the raving discontent of my party brethren. On our side, it is the diminishing caribou in Alaska, the hapless birds that get sucked into the wind turbines, the tainted voting machines, and, of course, the inflammatory talent of the other party. One balding fellow, I swear, spoke for virtually the entire meeting, pausing only to distribute his fliers for this cause and that, and of course, concluding on the note of his dramatic conversation with the Governor. The *patrones* were polite in their silence as he expounded, and I did my best to signal to them that he did not speak for me. Ours was a dispirited bunch, united in our national defeat, but people did have flattering things to say about my recent loss. The way I would walk the length of their gravel road in the height of summer just to meet them personally, and so forth. I wanted to immediately clarify that I have a glitch that way, there being some kind of deprivation involved, in the same way that I could recite from memory each of the dozen attendees' street addresses and precinct numbers.

But I kept silent. For a newcomer, I certainly did know the district by now, and I naturally wondered if perhaps my time would be better spent in some more meaningful pursuit, such as learning a foreign language. Or taking dance lessons. But as distracting as our free-flowing discussion proved to be, and as ill-suited as I probably am for this role, I realized that I felt at home in this unhappy and frantic room. The alternatives of inaction or traitorous affiliation might be tempting, as the balding Precinct Chair continued to lecture us on the meaning of our crushing presidential defeat; but I could always take solace in knowing that these meetings would ultimately come to an end.

I volunteered to be Ward Chair and to recruit others into the effort, my lone remaining sign drooping into the ditch off El Prado Street. And I also knew that the other side's equivalent must be *much worse*—their conversation safe within their own walls, in the sanctuary of their daily hatred—though surely in those meetings there were some who felt out of place as well. I just wanted to win the goddamned election, which is why I walked like I did throughout the months, with my talking points and my photo-shopped teeth. Of course, with this same energy I could have done something else: volunteer at a homeless shelter, go to couples counseling with Catherine, raise thousands for Hope House, or just play blackjack with my friends.

But it had been the political season, and I could not resist the siren call of the game.

34

Manuel ultimately became my sign-warrior, clued in to exactly where hers were versus mine. Strange, that phenomenon: trying not to be distracted by what the visible eye can see, and of course it's even worse when your distressed supporters are convinced that yard signs are the difference between victory and defeat. "How come you don't have any signs up? I see hers *everywhere*." Okay, already, let's do sign wars. And then I will *try not* to pull over, hammer in hand, just to match the opposition's presence, as it becomes contagious. And then that dopey phrase everywhere, what my campaign team came up with: *the road to a brighter tomorrow,* so wildly original. There are so many households, especially in the opposition's turf, up in the Bluffs: desert homes, comfortable, and with views of the city below, including my own adopted demesne with its roaming dogs and centuries of tradition. These neighborhoods, on the other hand, were brand new, and its residents were polite and amiable, even if they were Republican.

"Sorry to bother you," I began, as she emerged with phone in hand. "But I am running for State Senator, and I wanted to introduce myself personally to you."

"Well, hello," she said, cutting off the phone. "Now what's that again?"

"My name is Chapman Murphy. And I am running for the State Legislature."

"Nice to meet you," she said, extending her hand.

"Likewise," I replied. "This is a campaign piece of mine that has everything you would ever want to know about me. And *then some.*"

"Oh, that's fine," she laughed, looking over my flier. "What would you do if you got elected?"

"First of all," I began, "you would know who your State Senator is. Starting with this conversation." I paused. "Do you know who your State Senator is?"

"No, I don't."

"Well, in fairness to my opponent—who shall remain nameless, of course, at my campaign manager's urging—this *is* a new neighborhood. Less than two years, right?"

"January of last year," she replied, after mulling it over, "and most of the other homes around here too."

"There you go," I replied. "It's your first election, right? I mean here?"

"Yes," she replied, growing concerned. "But I don't know where I'm registered. Have I registered here?" she asked, looking at my clipboard.

"Yes, you have. Ms. Locklear?"

"That's right."

"You're on my sheet, see?" I raised my clipboard. "I know everything about you."

"What's on there?" Her eyes narrowed.

"I'm just kidding," I answered quickly. "But it does say here that you are an independent-minded voter who might go for the person rather than the party."

"Okay. I'm a registered Republican. But I *do* vote for the person."

"All right, then," I continued. "As you have probably figured out by now, I am a Democrat."

"Okay, I guessed as much. Why should I vote for you?"

"Well," I began, "apart from being accessible, because that only goes so far. Though it's a big far. We have to do better with our public schools. Families shouldn't be penalized for keeping their kids in the public system."

"Mine are in private. And we're going to stay like that. The gangs …"

"I know."

"But it is a financial strain. Even though my husband and I both work, have good jobs."

"All I am saying is that you *at least* have the viable option of staying in the public school system. I am a product of public schools myself, and I know what it's like to be behind everyone else. Like when I was in college."

"Did you grow up here?" she asked.

"No. Iowa."

"Oh, really?" her face brightened. "We're from Missouri."

"Just across the river, then. Do you like it here?"

"We're still getting used to it. But you can't beat the climate. I just don't like the mentality. How they do things. The way a person can have sixteen DWIs and still have their license."

"DWI is a real problem in this state."

"And the gangs," she continued. "What do *you* do?"

"I have been very fortunate to have been able to make service my vocation here in New Mexico I am a co-founder of a well-regarded local charity named Hope House."

"Oh, that's impressive."

"We work with ex-felons. We're like a halfway house. And over ninety percent of our residents do not commit new felonies and therefore do not end up back in the state correctional system."

"It must be hard work," she said in a kind of non-committal tone.

"It's a good program. And all about public safety, really. It's a safer ... what is the name of this street?"

"Hawthorn."

"Hawthorn Street. If someone doesn't re-offend."

"Well, hopefully they don't live around here to begin with. No offense."

"None taken. Rest assured that our facility is far away from here, down in the Valley."

"What else would you do? Besides start halfway houses?"

"Actually, I am deeply concerned about the availability of health care in this state. How can we afford to have one-quarter of our population uninsured?"

"Is it that few?" she asked. "From the stories I read, it seems like much more than that."

"And there again, the taxpayer like you ultimately assumes that burden. The same way with the Corrections tab. It costs at least thirty thousand dollars a year to house an inmate."

"Well, *that's* not good."

"No, it isn't. I would work towards relieving this burden. I want to be a burden reliever."

"Well, that *is* good," she laughed. "I should probably get back to my phone conversation, but it was nice of you to come around." She extended her hand.

"Will you consider voting for me?"

"I will consider it," she said, after a pause.

"*Keep me in mind,* as we say?"

"Okay then, I will. I will keep you in mind."

This was typical with the Ms. Locklears of the Bluffs. My campaign manager wanted me to be more on script, hitting the main bullet points with every potential voter, but I had to be myself. It was sales, though—that was evident to me from day one—and you had to read each situation to make any progress. With a Ms. Locklear, was I supposed to ask for her undying allegiance, right there at the end? Was I supposed to say, with total self-assurance, "Can I count on your support?" But that just seemed way too presumptuous to me. For starters, she was a Republican. And we had just met. How depressing it would be if she, or anyone else that matter, would *simply* vote for me on the basis of a three-minute conversation? But it was all about the numbers, as I would discover later, and I did try to follow up with personal notes to *all* of the Republicans I spoke with. I sent Ms. Locklear a note a few days later invoking her concern about gangs and DWI. My campaign manager liked *that* at least, even if it did not quite fit in with their standard methodology. If I wanted to sneak away for a church fiesta or some farmer's market morning, against their wishes, I was on my own there.

And speaking of being on my own, I give you the various confrontations I had with the dogs of District 10 over my five-month campaign. The first time I was bitten was totally my fault, part of my learning curve, as I went into the fenced yard despite the half-full food bowl and accompanying bowl of water. Around the corner of the house there suddenly appeared a blue heeler who went straight for my ankle. Its teeth were making progress through my socks when the homeowner mercifully appeared. "Jupiter didn't bite you, did he?" the man asked, after he had called the dog off. "He most definitely did," I answered, feeling my ankle and the wetness of blood starting to appear. "Are you sure?" he asked. "Yes, I am sure,' I answered curtly but politely. "I assume he has had his shots?" I continued. "Oh my, yes. We are good about those kinds of things. He's really a good dog. You just surprised him." I looked at Jupiter's owner. He seemed responsible. "All right, I'll live. Here is my campaign literature. Can I count on your vote?" You had better vote for me, I thought to myself. "I'll look it over," he replied. "But yes, I am a Democrat."

From this encounter, I learned never to enter a gate without being certain that no canines abided there. Or as certain as you can be. The next incident was of a different sort: the voter's door opens, and a dog suddenly emerges and goes straight for your wrist. That was my next unfortunate encounter. It was a little dog, too, the blood running down my arm, and a very apologetic woman who did not question whether or not I had really been bitten. She was a registered Republican, so I took that as one important vote gained.

Finally, there were the wandering dogs of the Valley, my Democratic stronghold—especially in the more rural parts of the district, dirt roads, unfenced lots. This was an inherently trickier situation, as no visible owner would be around. I still do not know exactly how to behave when in that critical moment, when it is just you and the growling dog, eye contact. Do you freeze, motionless, and try not to show any fear? Is it similar to confronting a bear when camping? In this case, I lucked out, as the German Shepherd's teeth did not break the skin, it was distracted by another dog fifty yards away. On I went to the next house.

Looking back on my vocational life before I ran for office, I am struck by just how many times Leroy Flowers saved us. There was that very high-profile crime, for instance—very ugly, execution style, several shopkeepers murdered in cold blood—but not done by any of our people. However, one of our residents had ties to the murderer, had done a previous crime with him, and the next thing we knew we had TV stations calling us, the newspaper, etc., wanting to know more about our Hope House resident named Sean Welch, who had been quietly going about constructing a positive, crime-free life within our programmatic walls. Given the intensity of the crime, its ruthless nature, any headline with "Hope House" in boldface posed a real threat to our very existence. Sean was embarrassed by it all. He truly was a one-time offender, and he was doing very well learning plumbing as a trade. But naturally we deflected all such media inquiries and had an emergency board meeting. Leroy was asked to step in and talk to the newspaper, and all three television stations.

And of course, he did. We brokered an understanding that Sean would be made available to speak on background about his one-time co-offender on the condition that they kept his name, and our name, out of the story. Whatever Leroy had said obviously worked, though my suspicion was that when they realized it was *Leroy Flowers* in their office, it was probably enough. Sean gave them what they wanted, always making it clear that he hardly knew the guy, and back to work he went.

35

There was little to soften how much money I needed to be competitive in my race, and situations inevitably emerged that were compromising by their very nature. Or at least potentially. I kept telling my campaign manager I would do *call time*, as he looked at my increasing unpaid balance, but the doors seemed a much more effective way to spend a candidate's time. The pressure I usually felt to raise money for Hope House had now been transferred to my own political ambition. For instance, I should mention that Adonis is a nationally known jazz musician, and is always on tour *somewhere,* socking away the cash. I had to ask him for a contribution: I was asking everyone else, so wouldn't I ask him? Even if it jeopardized our friendship, a complicated one where I had to proceed cautiously.

"Why should I give you any money?" he bristled, awaiting our next turn on the basketball court. "You don't even know what your positions are."

"What do you mean?" I replied defensively.

"We've talked about this. You just want a damned fancy license plate. And it suits some part of your odd psyche to do this."

"Not true. I might have joked about it in the past, but I'm sincere about it now. People have real problems ... and they need to be represented."

"And you're the guy?"

"I would at least like the chance."

"I am not sold," he replied, whipping his dreadlocks as he turned to catch a wayward basketball.

"Look," I said, "this is hard. You have to suddenly learn all of this *minutia.*"

"It's not minutiae. It's called policy."

"Okay," I began, in the way of a quiz, "what do you think about drilling in the Atrisco Reserve?"

"I think it is a bad idea," Adonis responded quickly. "Studies on the extent of oil reserves there are not conclusive. The potential for environmental damage is real—"

"Okay," I cut him off. "Bad example." Adonis shrugged. "How about this: do you favor making the State Board of Education a cabinet level office?" I continued. "And if so, why? And if not, why not?"

"More oversight would be a good thing," he began. "I don't have the figures before me, but we all know the problems facing the public schools in this state."

"How about Native monuments?" I continued. "Should we expand the freeway through them?"

"It's not a freeway," he answered. "A more accurate description would be an access road."

"Whatever."

"Look," he said impatiently, "I am not the one running for office."

"Why don't you?"

"Because I have a life," he continued. "And people like you will do it instead."

"That's why I need your money. You can be in my inner circle."

"Oh, really?" He laughed. Then he resumed his serious manner. "Listen, I don't like talking about these matters when I am at the gym. Especially money issues." His expression was growing more neutral. "I've got a major concert in Kyoto next week."

"When will you be back?"

"Why do you want to know?"

"Let me take you to lunch when you get back?"

"You don't eat lunch."

"Well, I would make an exception. In your case, that is."

"I don't know, dude." He shrugged again.

"Just think about it."

"Sure."

The game ended and we took the court. Adonis's presence on my team usually stressed me out, as he seemed to be so clued into my performance. Still, he was brutish underneath the basket, and for a musician, we marveled at his skill. And we worried about his hands, especially his fingers, as his trumpet was his livelihood. I think we won a couple of games that day, and I hit enough shots to keep him off my back. Of course, he never did contribute to my campaign— which was fine with me, to be honest. But he did seem to be genuinely pained months later when, upon his return from some European tour, I informed him that I had lost. "Damn," he said.

About the same time as my ill-fated request from Adonis, I was probably showing the strain of my campaign. Emily was upset with me because I could not stay awake during our evening phone calls, and I was losing weight that I did not have to begin with. I was definitely worried about what the opposition had on me, and Mike Powell was maddening in his inscrutability, elevating neutrality to an art form (only neutral because it was me, his friend). I was certain that I had an outstanding warrant buried in the courthouse, or official deadlines that I had missed. And there was always the business of having changed my address before the last eligible day before the election. And my partisan affiliation, from Independent to Democrat. And then there was what they could dig up about my time with Hope House: between unhappy former residents and disgruntled ex–board members. I was sure that accusations could be made, born out of rumor but not good to be aired. My bachelor status was a curveball, I suppose, and at least the diminutive union guy had been honest with me on that front.

Meanwhile, through it all, I had to remind myself why I was doing this. Actually, I was learning the reason the more I did it. Adonis had a good point, but that was towards the beginning of my campaign. That book on Robert Kennedy was buried somewhere in my car, which if I could find it would provide at least a moment of inspiration. In that book is a photo of him, black and white, crouching on the edge of some Appalachian ravine, junked car in the background, listening very intently to a barefoot five-year-old. The suit was tapered to his smallish frame, his shoes New England all the way, and yet he seemed at home with this little girl in her ragged attire, hearing her out, wanting to help. This man from another world of privilege and education. The more I spoke about the gift of service from the campaign stump—even in my modest world of State Senate District 10, not remotely on *his level*—the more fitting it became that he should be my hero. I remember several times trying to find that rumpled book in my car, but the memory of that photo was enough.

On the deepest level these things mattered: leaving the tower in his princely suit, submitting to the hopes of others, and then shouldering them as best he could. Plus, he had all of those children, relying upon him, waiting for him to come home from work. I, of course, did not have such a problem. And who am I, not even an elected official of a modest state office? And no prep school for this guy. But service is all I have, really. This love of my desolate adopted home with all of its problems, the longing that I encountered on the district streets that I walked until my shoes gave out. My hyped presence at your door. Always the notion that we could do better—what my Republican parents had taught me—and that the only reason for wealth is the grace in owning up to its responsibility. To give back. Wealth has a capacity to effect societal change, our collective potential that needs to be fiercely pursued. Especially now, in the face of that one television channel and its numerous radio cousins.

36

It was probably a good thing, in only one way, that my father had passed before he would have had to process me running for public office as a Democrat. The choices in my life were baffling enough to him, and certainly my political affiliation was on that list. Working with ex-convicts was another. And now, running for the State Legislature as a *Democrat?* As I mentioned earlier, I stopped going home for the various holidays and reunions years ago. Still, if he had been alive, given the pressure of my monthly campaign bill to my consultants, I probably would have gone back home to Iowa to ask him for money. As I understood it, that is what political candidates often do to meet the financial demands, start with their own family.

I would have, and it probably would have gone like this:

"So," he says, his office door strangely open, "what brings *you* here?" His manner is familiar and immediately evokes numerous unwanted memories.

"Well," I began, "I am a part of this family. Do I have to have a reason to come home?"

"Beats me," he fires back. "We never hear from you. You don't answer your phone."

"I've explained that to you. I get these calls from inmates … their mothers, or girlfriends. I just don't answer the phone. But I do get back to you, eventually."

"No, you don't," he replies in an unsettling neutral tone. "I don't care how you live your life," he continues. "You're an adult."

"Okay."

"What do you want?"

"Well," I reply, sensing how doomed this whole situation is. "As you know, I am running for the State Senate where I live."

"I should tell you right now I am not giving you a dime."

"Okay … um, is there a reason?"

"A reason?" he laughs. "You made that decision on your own. Why should I help you out?"

"Do you have any idea how much money I have to come up with?" I answer, beginning to get angry.

"So? Get the people who encouraged you to do this to back you."

"It's *so much* money. Candidates often begin with their families, it's so much. I need like thirty-five thousand dollars by October."

"Do what others do, your fellow Democrats. How do other people raise the necessary funds?"

"Like I said," I answer sarcastically. "They often begin with their own family."

"You should have thought about this beforehand."

"Well, I've already made the commitment," I sigh. "I'm living it. Have the best campaign team … it's very public at this point. I am the Democratic nominee for Senate District 10."

"How can you be a Democrat?" he asks, his forehead beginning to redden with anger. "You've had all of these benefits."

"Wait a second," I reply.

"Weren't you asked to run as a Republican two years ago? Your brother said as much. That they had a district for you and everything? A shoo-in."

"I definitely regret telling him that. Thought I could confide in Fred."

"Why in the hell didn't you take it? You want to be up there so bad? You wouldn't have to be begging people for money."

"Well, for starters, I am not a Republican. How can I run as a Republican if I am not a fucking Republican?"

"Do not use that kind of language in my office."

"I can't pretend to be somebody that I am not."

"It's a choice you made. Live with it."

"You want to know why I'm a Democrat?" I reply, my anger starting to take over. "I'll tell you why: I was walking a precinct a few weeks back, and I had this great conversation with this fellow. Joe Gallegos. He was out in his driveway working on his truck. Nice neighborhood—affluent by standards out there. Anyway, he starts talking about how his other business-owner friends goad him about his politics. He said tax-wise he has plenty of reason to vote Republican, that he takes a beating that way. But then he says to me, "You know what I tell them? These friends of mine? I am one of seven children, and we grew up poor. One of my sisters, she's on public assistance right now. She's had lots of problems. Do you think the Republicans give a *damn* about her? *That's* why I'm a Democrat,' he tells me." I look at my father, who seems to have been paying attention. "You guys lack a sensitivity to the world around you," I continue. "Your reality just isn't my reality."

"We differ there," he answers coolly. "There is suffering in the world. But his sister should get a job, try to improve her lot. Make something of herself."

"Sometimes it's more *complicated* than that."

"What would you know about being poor?" he replies. "That's my territory. We had to take in boarders, invite strangers into our house. It was the Depression. I've worked hard to get where I am today. And you've benefited from that, Mister."

"You don't think it's important to give back?" I counter.

"People should take responsibility for their lives," he replies. "Starting in your case. You should have had a plan before you decided to do this. In business we make such evaluations before we act."

"Okay. I have learned. But I can't reverse my decision. It's all playing out in front of *everyone.*"

"That's not my problem," he says coldly.

"No, it isn't your problem."

"I just think you're used to people making excuses for themselves. Like these criminals you work with."

"Now wait a second. They take responsibility for their lives. They *have* to. They're on fucking parole."

"Your language?" he says firmly.

"Fine."

"I don't know about that world. But I could give you a sob story too. Do you have *any* idea what it was like for my parents to make ends meet? I remember that sack of potatoes that sustained us for a month."

"How ethnically perfect," I interject, trying to inject *some* levity into our conversation.

"Yeah?" he replies, smiling momentarily. "I suppose so." Then he resumes his lecturing tone. "Well, you can make light of it if you want."

"I am *not* making light of it."

"And when I became an *adult,*" he continues, "I looked around, and everyone had more than I did. But I didn't make excuses. I just decided to work harder than everyone else, those people with their privileges and prep schools. Like you and your brothers."

"I didn't go to prep school. Remember?"

"Well, maybe you should have," he says, without humor. "Then maybe you'd appreciate your advantages. Or at least you wouldn't be working with a bunch of criminals. For that *salary* of yours."

"Yeah? Maybe I'd be married too?"

"That's your business."

"With kids? Living here?"

"You've made your choices."

"Fine," I answer.

"Wherever that is where you live, you must like it out there. Running for the State Legislature. We're here in Iowa. Why should we care?"

"You shouldn't. Forget it, then."

"What is your request? Finish your sentences."

"Ah, the hell with it. We both know where this is going."

"I promised your mother I'd hear you out."

"Fine, then. I need to raise thirty-five thousand dollars by October first."

"*Thirty-five thousand* dollars? Is that what you are asking me for?"

"It's just a request, okay? I do this for a living, believe it or not. Ask people for shit."

"You should clean up your language, Mister. You might have more success."

"Fine. Are we done?"

"I've got nothing else," he answers, shrugging his shoulders.

"I'm just on my own, man," I say bitterly, rising up from the chair. "Just like I've always been. Forget it. I'll see you back at the house."

"Make sure you're there for dinner. Your mother is very excited to have you here."

"Great," I answer. "It's great to be here," I add. "What a fucking place." I slam his office door shut.

The irony of the above imaginary scenario, which actually has much lived experience in it, is that my father probably would have given me the money. But only after a scene like this. Among his many qualities, he liked to surprise. Accordingly, I could see him quietly mailing a $35,000 check made out to my campaign a couple of weeks later, after I had given up hope, along with a note saying, "*Just win the race, buster. And never ask me for money again.*" Something like that. He loved me, deep down. And I loved him.

Of course, I still had the problem of the thirty-five thousand dollars. That was real. I could ask the board of Hope House for a one-time bonus, as a start, I thought at the time, for my years of service, but that would be inappropriate for at least seven different reasons. Then there were my unpaid loans to various Hope House residents, back when I did not know any better. But repayment on *that* front would be truly laughable. Emily had no money. I could not exactly sublet the apartment that I had eventually found in the district, as I did need a place to live.

I was desperate. My campaign manager needed payment in advance before our final mailings could go out. And there was their monthly fee to consider as well, plus the cost of signs and billboards and the strangely vital yet extremely expensive polling. He had given me a budget, complete with colored timetables and monthly estimated costs. Thirty-five thousand dollars was what they needed.

Then it came to me: *Mr. O'Connor.*

Not just him, of course, but his *network*. I did not look forward to this kind of ask, as it seemed way overboard, pushing it, to say the least. But then I remembered that he too had run for the State Legislature, decades back. And he had lost. The hard thing would be to make the actual request. I would need to have a promising horoscope that week, and just the right amount of caffeine. Afternoon sunlight streaming into his law office would help as well.

But in the meantime, my job was to continue campaigning, to walk, as I have indicated, and walk I did. Until I was half-giddy with street names and secrets of the animal kingdom. Not just dogs. There was a colony of bees that I came to be familiar with, on this one particular street—there, in a friendly tree. Roadrunners occasionally flitted by, especially in the Bluffs, where there was more open space. And the sound of locusts, back in my wooded home turf of the Valley, it being late July.

There was always a list of insurmountable tasks for me, the candidate, to do. Daily, weekly, monthly. Go recruit fifty volunteers by next week. Assign them phone nights or walk weekends. Answer this questionnaire on your environmental positions by Tuesday. Raise thirty-five thousand dollars. Do your follow-up letters to contacted Republicans by Saturday. Make these fund-raising calls. Meet with the trial-lawyer guy, and then do your audition for the Progressive Democratic PAC. Raise thirty-five thousand dollars. Line up specific testimonials from the following individuals for your next three mailings by Monday of next week, and make sure that their words of praise for you are not redundant. Raise thirty-five thousand dollars.

I grew to hate my campaign manager's voice on the phone,

and I suspect the feeling was mutual. But I did learn that, in this phase of my life, I absolutely *had* to answer the phone or suffer the consequences.

37

It was time to check on our funding request, as there was less than a week remaining in the session. My instinct said zero in on O'Rourke, if I could coax him away from his more consequential clients and do everything he says. At this point there was little reason to bring our Hope House emissaries with me, as presumably the case had already been made. There was no shortage of ways to spend the public dollar, however, and so many worthy projects to fund.

"Hey, dawg." That voice. And yet incongruous, to be heard here in the marble hallways of our State Capitol. I turned around, and it was him.

"Donald!" I exclaimed. "What are *you* doing here?"

"I just thought you could use some backup," he replied. "With these kinds of folks up here." He was still wearing those black glasses of his, though he did seem a bit thinner.

"Are you still on parole?"

"Nope." He laughed that signature laugh. "They cut me out early. My p.o. said he was tired of wasting his time on me. That the state had better ways to spend its money."

"Well, that's appropriate," I interrupted. "Because that's what we're doing here. We're in trouble, guy."

"I told you. We don't have to pay *salaries*."

'We just missed on a couple of grants," I protested. "Macey's good with that. Otherwise we'd be fine."

"Does the board know?" Donald asked.

"Yes. Mike Powell is around here somewhere, but we have a real shot at this funding. Want to tag along?"

"Heck yeah."

"Are you off work?"

"I'm actually on vacation, dawg. … Mr. Scott said he didn't want to see me for a whole week."

"That's great."

"I thought I'd come up and find you. Colter told me you'd be here. And since I'm off paper now, I figured, why not?"

"Excellent. Now come with me."

O'Rourke was just around the corner, as it turned out. But he was completely engrossed with at least one legislator and a couple other of lobbyists. Just a glimpse from him and I knew he would give us some time, nevertheless. One thing about being with Donald, we made for a visible duo. And in his company, I was always strangely confident.

"Are you still with Emily?" Donald asked, as we waited for O'Rourke to finish his conversation.

"Yes."

"I am sure I don't need to tell you this, but she is beautiful."

"I know," I answered quickly. "Or, I mean, *thanks.*"

"You two are a lot alike. It would be unfortunate if you lost her."

"I *know,*" I replied. "Why are you telling me this?"

Donald shrugged. "I just worry about you, dawg … that's all."

"Worry about Hope House. Or yourself even, for a change?"

"I'm making improvements that way."

"Remember our pledge? *Me first.*"

"Yeah. *Me first.*"

"Enough of this self-sacrifice," I continued, "and taking care of others. Are you still visiting Velma at Grants?"

"I can't help it, dawg. I promised her I would."

"But she's *in prison.* Violated her parole big time. In a flagrant way, if I remember right."

"She's got a reconsideration hearing coming up. She doesn't have anybody else."

I paused, then looked at my friend directly: *"Me first. Remember?"*

"I'm trying ... I really am."

At that moment, O'Rourke released his audience and was moving our way. "Hey there," he said. "This your friend?" O'Rourke asked, looking at Donald.

"Yes," I answered.

"Walk with me, you two." And we did. O'Rourke was moving swiftly, especially for a man in his seventies. "Did you talk with the Pro Tem?"

"Yes," I replied.

"What did he say?"

"That he would do what he can."

O'Rourke was not pleased with this information. "You have got to pin him down. Tell him there is language in the Corrections Budget that would make this extremely easy."

"I told him about that," I clarified.

"You've got to pin him down. The train has maybe already left the station, but you can still get on."

"Can Senator Cohen help?"

"Sure," he replied. "You never know. But work it." He had reached his destination. O'Rourke turned around. "What's your friend's name?"

"Donald," Donald answered. "I was in the Hope House."

"He set a record for the longest stay so far," I interjected. "What, fourteen months?" I asked Donald.

"Seventeen," he replied.

"It's a good program," O'Rourke said. "It needs to be funded," he added with finality.

"Okay, thanks," I said, as he vanished into his numerous other high-powered doings.

As always, Donald's presence affected me—in this case, his advice about Emily. For her part, my obsession with getting elected remained a mystery to her during the long months of the campaign. It had definitely put a strain on our relationship. How could it not? There was that night, for example, when a group of young professional women applauded when we entered the restaurant, and she knew it was not for her, that she was only a footnote (that is what she *thought,* at least). Or the night that party operative had her legs too close to mine, or at least Emily thought so. And of course, there were my relapses into flirtation, while Emily was off in the ladies' room, which were real and undeniable, as she came back to the table full of accusation, asking why I felt the need to get the waitress's phone number like that, et cetera. It is fairly embarrassing, when I reflect upon that behavior now; and if I could make it up to her, I would.

But, on a different subject, my visit with Mr. O'Connor went like this:

"Hi there, sir."

"Chapman. Always pleasant to see you," he answered. He buzzed his secretary to hold his phone calls.

"Sir— "

"Call me Joseph. We are on that level now."

"Okay, Joseph. First of all, I want to thank you again for picking up the check at the Country Club. That was above and beyond. And for all of us at Hope House, *thanks.*"

"It was my pleasure. Turned out to be kind of an expensive dinner for me," he laughed softly. "Didn't it?"

"You've got that right," I smiled.

"But it was worth it. Reggie's story really touched me. How is he doing, anyway?"

I paused. "Actually, not so well. He relapsed not long after the benefit, and I think he is doing the rest of his parole inside."

Mr. O'Connor's expression changed. "I am sorry to hear that."

"But that is how it goes with many of our residents. It's a long road. Our job is to present the opportunity for a different life to them. Sometimes it doesn't take the first go-round."

"I understand. Jesus spoke often about this very same thing. We must always forgive. And be aware of the least of our brothers and sisters."

I hesitated. "Agreed."

"How is your campaign going?" he continued.

"Pretty good. Our polling indicates that we have a real shot."

"I told you that I ran for the State Legislature once, right?"

"Yes, you did."

"I lost." He smiled. "It was a bad year for Democrats."

"Were you close?" I asked.

"Not really," he replied. "I probably would have lost anyway. What brings you here today?"

I gathered my thoughts, tried to mule through my ambivalence about what I was going to ask. "Well, sir—"

"Joseph."

"Yes, Joseph. As you mentioned, I am not quite sure what kind of year this will be for Democrats. But I am very much in the hunt for my race, down ballot, if you know what I mean?"

"That's good news," he nodded.

"Yes, it is. The problem is, these days, as you know, campaigns cost so much. My campaign team is confident that we can pull this off if we could do two or three more mailings."

"And those cost money, right?"

"Right."

"How much do you need?"

I drew a deep breath. "Thirty-five thousand dollars."

"From me?" he asked, somewhat incredulous.

"No, not just from you. I was thinking you might have some ideas on who I could ask? Colleagues of yours."

"Most of my colleagues are Republicans."

There was an awkward silence. Our eye contact had ceased. He was staring out his top story window, with its stunning view of our small metropolis. And the distant mountains.

"You know," he continued, "our state has a lot of problems. I try to do what I can."

"Of course, you do, sir." I interjected hurriedly. "I mean Joseph."

He looked at me directly, his gentle eyes surveying whatever I presented at that moment. "Young man, you remind me of what I might have done if my life had taken a different direction. Those days were different. You got married, started a family, found employment to support all of that. I could have gone in your direction. I might have."

There was silence between us.

"Let me see what I can do," he finally said.

"I know it's a lot of money."

"It's only money. You do good work. How should the checks be made out?"

"Chapman Murphy for District 10."

"Okay. Sounds good. Give me a couple of days."

"I don't know what to say, I answered, catching myself. "Joseph."

"Just do your best to win that race, okay?" he smiled. Echoes of my father.

"For sure I will. Do my best that is."

Eight days later, the checks arrived—a group of them, in an envelope, mostly bearing the last name "O'Connor"(he had a big family), but not all of them. They met my total request. I sat in my car, near the apartment mailboxes including my own, for a long time. Then I realized that I should get to my campaign consultant's office. But the bank first. ASAP.

Emily really did hang in there with me—with that child's voice of hers that gives me goose bumps when I think of it. Like an invitation into the better parts of my own childhood. She was so … *alluring* that way. And she had done such an excellent job with our hotel suite victory spread on election night. The early news was good. My volunteers were there, hopeful, and I was there, the candidate, presenting a confident front. My campaign manager was enmeshed in numbers, and his expression was less encouraging as the evening progressed. Then his countenance became even more troubling as the unavoidable hope began to unravel. But we tried *not* to let on in front of the odd assortment of guests, who were glued to the national race anyway. The evening had continued to darken, both micro and macro, and I had to somehow not retreat into irony and random comments. It was all so sad—the hope in their faces, my people, and the unwillingness to abandon that hope. There was one precinct yet to be heard from and anything was possible mathematically, until once again my campaign manager's visage shadowed the room. Someone, perhaps it was me, said: "Buzz-killer, go away." And the others joined in, in a teasing and cathartic way. *Yeah, buzz-killer, why are you such a buzz-killer?* And so on, with different variations. He took it well, as he knew we were beaten, and he shook my hand in the hotel hallway in a way that I will never forget. "It has been a pleasure," he said with unaccustomed formality, both of us starting to become emotional. "Likewise," I responded, curtly, as if both of us had suddenly gone military. And then he went off to his numbers, and his other races.

I really needed to be with Emily that night—after the guests had left, after we had managed a subdued commiseration in the impending realization of what was to be. The one elder newscaster held out until early morning, reluctant to crown our reigning president again, and we held out as well in our top floor room. Earlier in the evening some party official had asked me to go downstairs and make a speech, along with the other unsuccessful candidates, but there was no way I could pretend that losing was no big deal. My dis- associative powers were not on *that* level. Also, I did not want to disappoint all of these good people in our room, as a host, munching on cake and bad pasta salad. And certainly, the larger picture was much more important, much more troubling than my local race. We were making the best of it, having chased away our buzz-killer, my campaign manager. Of all the somber parties that night, ours was the best—from all reports.

When I turned to Emily at 2:00 a.m. with chocolate and champagne, my need was fierce. It is not as if I have any motive to embellish or inflate my amorous powers—I hate it when men do that. Rest assured that I know solitude and its insecurity intimately, and at this point in my life why pretend otherwise? But I needed to have Emily that night, especially so, and, consistent with the dynamic between us, she wanted me, too. We made love well into the next morning—wildly—as what else is there to do in these situations but to take solace in each other's bodies?

And then with morning, such an awful realization: my loss, his loss, *our* loss. The party balloons withering in defeat, my new campaign operative friends looking dispirited as they found their cars in the harsh morning light. The one young woman, I do not remember her name, devoted to change at the top—and everything truly *was* at stake, or so it seemed—

there she was, walking to her car, an armload of hopeful posters and get-out-the-vote fliers, alone in her surprise, the Republicans the reigning party of dark maturity. All of those young people that suddenly appear—for us candidates—working hard on our behalf, believing in a better world, which will be *their* world someday. Then to the breakfast café, where people like us congregate, and the sadness of *everyone*. Mutterings about moving to Canada, ballot machines, and then for me the realization that I had lost slowly sinking in. All of that effort. But a free cappuccino on the house, and the tearful barista. Emily and I quietly holding hands, such a good girlfriend as she never truly understood the why-for of this. Why on earth *does* one run for office? Only to get beaten by the predicted voter performance percentage, no matter how I had walked and strived.

38

When I spotted Carlos from a distance, it was just intuition to risk interrupting him. As with O'Rourke, he had major contracts and obligations to fulfill in these waning days of the short session. When he saw me though, he motioned me to come over, which I took as a good sign.

"Chappie," he began, "you are in luck. Methinks you are in the budget." He smiled.

"*No,*" I replied, reluctant to invite the cruelty of hope.

"Methinks you are. I spoke with the Pro Tem."

"For reals?"

"For reals."

"For how much? The full amount?"

"Two hundred thousand dollars, what you asked for."

"With the emergency clause?"

"That too." I was truly surprised. "I don't know what to say."

"I told him about Hope House. I don't think he understood exactly what your program does. He's got family in that circumstance, though ... as many of us do."

"That is fantastic!" I exclaimed, as the reality of what Carlos was saying began to sink in.

"Your work's not over yet," he cautioned. "Now you get to the fourth floor and make sure the Governor doesn't line item—"

"For sure," I replied, my pulse quickening.

"Helping criminals is not exactly a popular position."

"Got it."

"But the appropriation does seem to be safely buried in the Corrections Budget."

"Should I tell Senator Cohen?"

He nodded. "Always good to have many eyes on these things."

"When does the Governor sign the budget?"

"Depends. He might want to just get it over with before we actually end the session."

"Okay."

"The Pro Tem didn't really know a whole lot about you. You need to get your name out more."

"Will do."

In a way, it is probably a good thing that I lost, as I really wondered if I could pull off the boundary thing. It would kill me if I had to disappoint Manuel, or Loyola, the bunch at the restaurant, if there was a vote they strongly disapproved of. Which would be inevitable, seeing as how we are from different worlds. Most of them go to Mass at 6:30 every morning. They are so polite to me—this odd stranger who wants to represent them in Santa Fe. I really would do anything for them in return, which is maybe not an ideal position to be in. In politics, I mean. I will not know, because I lost, but I do know that there is a hidden tradition perhaps still in play, even if it is largely a memory: the transactional approach, the strong-arming, or the cash contributions that I learned how to accept a few months back. All part of the game. The larger picture is that some of us are trying to make this a better world. And if it means being a Valley Democrat with all of its implications, so be it. The opposition can pounce on the purported shadiness of unions, for example, or the unpopular notion of preserving ancient Native monuments instead of improving traffic flow. But at least some of us are trying. *Their* solution is to take personal responsibility to its extreme.

Certainly, my own father would not have been amused to have heard my speech before Electrical Workers Local 59, as I went on about the right to a meaningful wage. I can say that from an early age in my family we were taught that unions were the worst things ever; they were *bad,* irresponsible blockages to the flowering of free enterprise. It was my dad's fault, really, because if he wanted me to turn out like I did, more attention needed to be paid. Slipped through the cracks, alert always to the exit door I was. And I was comfortable before Electrical Workers Local 59, despite my narrow vintage tie and my karaoke reference when handed the microphone that was not understood. How *much* an hour for the minimum wage? Hell, why not twenty?

Towards the end of the campaign it must have been clear to others that I was not quite right. I could fix upon certain houses, or precincts, for example. When I would exclaim: "God, how I *love* Precinct 10!" after getting my walk sheet, my campaign manager would look at me, puzzled. "What do you mean by that?" he would ask. "These are votes that we are collecting here. Numbers." And I would reply, "Yes, but certain sections of the district are more interesting than others. " Such answers would seem to satisfy him, at least temporarily. What I neglected to tell him was that there were certain trees I was fond of in Precinct 17, for example— gnarled, dead, twisted oaks—and that I could replenish myself by gazing at them. Then it was off to another street, my car ignition barely functioning at this point, but certainly, the cute schoolteacher's house merited another visit before I called it an evening. I had my own personal reasons for doing this, or surviving this—an affinity maybe, with the prospect of fitting in *somewhere*.

No matter how compelling the *other* more emotional reasons are for doing this—the numbers are the numbers—and District 10 is gone, many say. So too, my intoxicating adventures into the targeted neighborhoods, maps and voter lists in hand. Always racing against the setting sun, as the objective was to personally meet *thousands* of people by the first Tuesday in November. I probably took this impossible goal too literally, but my campaign manager really did not know me before the whole goddamned thing started. He might have mentioned in passing that specific number to me in an exaggerated way—with his eye, of course, towards motivation—but again, he had no idea that I would take it seriously, literally. Because I was taught in my family that anything worth doing is *worth doing well.*

39

It was probably that episode with the waitress that clinched it for Emily: "I cannot do this anymore," she told me, tearfully, about a week after election night. We were alone in our favorite café.

"I can do better," I protested. "I *promise.*"

"I did not want to hurt your feelings during the campaign," she continued. "So, I waited until afterwards."

"You did such a great job with this ... very unusual situation."

"I don't think you understand," she said. Her tone was different than it had been in the past—more resolute, more resigned. "You are just too hard to be with."

"I'm sorry," I replied, meaning it.

"I gave it a chance," she continued. "More than a chance. But you have so *many* ... *issues* that you are reluctant to address."

"I really don't think that's true."

"I need to be with somebody I can trust. Or at least be comfortable with. ... You just present such a *challenge*—"

"No doubt your therapist agrees with this decision." She did not respond. "I really wish you would give this time," I continued. "The past year has been weird." I reached for her hand. Not much of a response.

"I know you've tried ... as I have tried. But our needs are so different."

"Not true. Really."

"You are just too much. You have hurt me in ways that no other man has before."

I did not know what to say at this point, as *the past* had always been a charged issue for us. And now, the reality was that Emily was planning to leave. California, going back to school. And now I would have the challenge of *moving on,* as they say. This will be difficult; I can see the outlines of that already. Trying not to spend the next few years looking for someone *just like her.* We seemed like a charmed couple from the start, despite our issues. There were so many reasons to be together, as Donald had mentioned. And now, will I have to carry her unfamiliar absence into my solitude? I am tempted to call her fairly constantly, in the spirit of persuasion, but I know that would be a bad idea. I should give her time. She needs space and all of that. But it is difficult to picture my life without her. It certainly has been a lesson as to the inevitable choices in life, and their consequences.

40

It was now time to make contact with the Governor before the crush of the session was over. This was not an easy task for me, as just being around him brought up all of my issues: authority, celebrity, the echo of my own father, et cetera. The whole logic of my own life has been to remain on the margins, staying close to the surface while the bigger fish position themselves in the depths. Certainly, diving deeper than usual presented certain risks. We needed to talk to him personally. I *hated* this, for reasons I have mentioned and because in general I am used to living on possibility. I would do anything for Hope House. I managed an appointment through his people that I had come to know during my campaign.

"How are you, Chapman?" the Governor asked, rising from his giant chair. His desk was similarly massive, the State Seal under glass, a phone on top.

"Fine, Governor. Except that it sucks to lose."

"Oh yes," he frowned. "You got—well, I should watch my language—*fucked.* You needed him to do better at the top. He owes you."

"I can't believe we lost the state," I replied. "I mean, there is no way we are a Red State."

"There's a lot of blame to go around," he said pensively. "We can certainly see it all in retrospect."

"It's nice of you take the time to meet with me. It must be crazy right now."

"Yes, it is," he answered, his manner changing slightly. "In fact, I've got another meeting in two minutes. What is it that you want?" He was now all business.

"You know the work that I do? With Hope House? The program for ex-felons?"

"Yes, I'm generally familiar with it."

"Well, we've done a great job over the years successfully reintegrating parolees—men and women—back into society."

"That's difficult work."

"Yes, it is. We have a lot of support up here, though. On both sides. We are in the Corrections Budget as a line item for two hundred thousand dollars. Of course, it will be an RFP. We are hoping that you will not veto it."

"What will you do with the money?"

"The extra funding will allow us to continue, maybe even expand. Possibly open a house here in Santa Fe—that is, if we can convince the neighborhood like we did in Albuquerque."

"Good luck on that front," he said, smiling. Then he looked at his watch. "That sounds fair enough. I'll alert my staff to leave it alone. It's difficult. Our state has so many needs, so many worthy causes."

"Oh, definitely."

"But yours is an important one." He got up from his chair. I did as well. "What are you going to do next?" he asked, extending his hand.

"Oh, I am definitely going to stay involved in politics." I resisted the temptation to call him *Guv.* "I just don't know about that district, though. I think it might be gone."

"Well, it could be. But you never know."

"I'll keep my options open."

"*Do* that. We'll help you any way we can."

"Thanks. I will keep you posted."

"You ran a good race. I hope you stay with it."

"Thanks," I said.

He put his arm on my shoulder. "The party needs people like you."

"I do not know what to say," I replied, shaking his hand. "About the appropriation."

"Just keep doing this good work of yours. Lord knows we need it."

That is all I have to relay at this point. I am forty-three years old. Rest assured that the weight of my fund-raising load continues, that I will probably relent and see a stupid therapist as Emily insisted, especially if it gives her a reason to reconsider the decision to leave me. Our Hope House alumni will continue to succeed and often relapse in consistent fashion, and in all probability, I will run again in District 10. I cannot help myself. I will forever be on the side of the line with Donald, Colter, Cesare and all of my Hope House alums, for whom life is problematic.

I am the strange bachelor walking down your street.